PRISONERS OF THE SEA

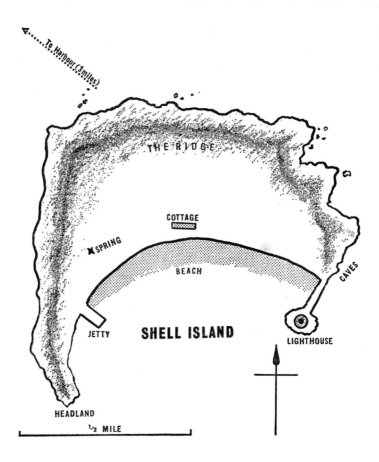

To Harbour.(3 miles)

THE RIDGE

COTTAGE

✕ SPRING

BEACH

CAVES

JETTY

SHELL ISLAND

LIGHTHOUSE

HEADLAND

½ MILE

PRISONERS OF THE SEA

by

DENNIS W. BOREHAM

VICTORY PRESS

LONDON and EASTBOURNE

© Dennis W. Boreham 1968

SBN 85476 002 4

For Peter

Printed in Great Britain for
VICTORY PRESS (Evangelical Publishers Ltd.),
Lottbridge Drove, Eastbourne, Sussex,
by Richard Cay (The Chaucer Press), Ltd.,
Bungay, Suffolk

CHAPTER 1

The summer holidays were half over and the first excitement of six weeks away from school was beginning to wear off. Peter's thoughts were far away from the piano he was playing so carelessly in the sitting-room. John was upstairs in the bathroom, humming a merry tune while he cleaned his teeth, pausing every so often to complete a few bars and trying hard not to swallow too much of the toothpaste he had squeezed on to his brush.

They had finished their breakfast a half hour ago. The next important event was the arrival of the mail. The brothers in their separate tasks were keeping a listening ear for the tell-tale sound of the front gate creaking, a sure sign of the postman's arrival at that time of the morning.

John heard the sound first. Not pausing to dry his face, he rushed from the bathroom and leapt down the stairs, which were well used to the battering the twins had given them over the years.

Peter ran from the sitting-room, leaving a trail of sheet music all over the carpet. He was just in time to collide with his brother as he jumped the last five stairs. They landed in a heap on the doormat. The postman, chuckling to himself, let the letters fall on top of them. He knew the boys well!

Peter rubbed his head and grabbed a couple of letters which had slipped off his back on to the floor. John was on his feet already with a bill in his hand.

He grinned broadly.

'One for Grandfather,' Peter said, 'and another one for us—from Janet and Ann!'

John dropped the bill and took the letter from his brother. He ran up the stairs into their bedroom. Peter, more quietly, took his grandfather's letter into the dining-room.

'Sorry! Can't stop!' he apologised. 'We have an important letter to read.'

Their grandfather gave a knowing smile and then winced as he heard Peter bound up the stairs and stride heavily across the bedroom floor.

John was sitting on his bed, reading intently.

'Let me have a look, then!' Peter protested. 'What do they say?'

'What do they say!' John shouted happily. 'Just read it and see!'

He thrust the letter into Peter's hand and leaned over his brother's shoulder to make sure he had not made a mistake.

'Dear Peter and John,' Peter read aloud. 'We are having a marvellous time down here at Sedgecombe. And guess what? Uncle says you can both come for a fortnight! And he owns an ISLAND! We can STAY ON IT! Come as soon as you can.'

The twins didn't wait to read any more. They shot out of the door, skidded on the landing carpet and hurtled through the hall. The cat rushed from the house in terror through the open kitchen door. Their mother was in the garden.

'Mum! What do you think?'

Peter's voice was shrill with excitement.

'We've had an invitation to go on holiday,' John explained, no less enthusiastically. 'Can we go?'

Peter pushed his brother, playfully.

'Silly!' he said. 'We haven't told Mum who has asked us, yet.'

Their mother paused in her task of hanging the washing on the line and dried her hands on her apron. Her eyes were full of laughter.

'Is home such an awful place that you want to rush away so quickly?' she chided.

'Oh, no!' John exclaimed. 'But at least Grandfather will have some peace!'

'And we have been home from school for three whole weeks,' Peter added. 'I'm sure you can do with a rest, too.'

Their mother laughed.

'You are very persuasive this morning,' she replied. 'But you are wasting your time. Your father and I spoke to Mr. Mortimer on the telephone yesterday. We think a holiday by the sea will do you both a lot of good.'

'So you knew all the time!' John exclaimed. 'We can go? You don't mind?'

Peter's face creased into a wide smile.

'Oh, thank you very much,' he said. 'Can we go to-morrow?'

Their mother nodded her head.

'Tomorrow,' she replied. 'I'll help you to pack.'

CHAPTER 2

It wasn't a Saturday when one would expect the greatest volume of passenger traffic, but Victoria Coach Station was thronged with travellers. And with coaches. There were coaches everywhere! Coaches of every colour and size, ready to speed through the length and breadth of England, and some abroad.

Peter glanced at his watch.

'We are nearly half an hour early,' he said, putting his case down.

John smiled.

'I'm glad we are early,' he replied. 'It will take us quite a time to find our coach.'

Peter looked around the vast garage.

'Look, there is an Inspector over there,' he said. 'I'll run across and see whether he can help us.'

The Inspector was very busy answering a host of enquiries from several bewildered travellers. Peter waited his turn patiently.

'Can you tell me where we catch the coach for Sedgecombe, please?' he asked, when the people in front of him had hurried away.

The Inspector looked through the sheaf of papers which were clippe.. to a board he carried.

'In the other garage,' he said. 'Through the archway, over the road and around the corner. Royal Blue. Have a good trip.'

Peter thanked him and returned to John.

'I'm glad I asked,' he said. 'We don't catch the coach from this garage. There is another garage over the road. It goes from there. Royal Blue.'

'Let's hurry, then,' John replied, picking up his luggage. 'We don't want to miss it!'

They threaded their way carefully through the people who were sitting on their cases because all available seats in the garage were occupied. They walked under the archway and crossed the road. There was a big sign which directed travellers to the other garage.

'Phew! That's better!' John exclaimed. 'There is loads of room in here.'

There were three Royal Blue coaches in the garage, and another helpful Inspector showed them which one to board. Quickly, they dumped their cases in the compartment at the rear of the coach and climbed aboard. They sat at the back.

The coach was soon filled. When the driver had checked their tickets and counted the people to make sure everyone was aboard, he slid the door to and started the engine. There was a sudden surge of power which travelled the full length of the vehicles and made the seats throb. The driver selected a gear and released the handbrake. The shining coach edged forward at a snail's pace, carefully avoiding the people who were criss-crossing their way about the garage. Glancing back, Peter noticed another coach moving already into the rank they had just left, ready to repeat the process they had gone through.

John squinted as the coach swung out of the garage into the bright sunshine which shone down upon the streets of London on that hot August morning.

'I hope the weather stays as fine as this,' he remarked.

The coach was delayed in the heavy traffic and, by

the time they passed the airport, they were ten minutes late. However, out of London at last, they sped down the motorway in fine style. When they reached Salisbury they were ahead of schedule.

They halted for twenty minutes at a restaurant where other coaches were parked. John looked at the queue for refreshments and decided not to join it.

'I want to save my pocket money for the holiday,' he said.

Peter agreed.

The rest of the journey seemed long. The country was pretty enough and quite hilly, but the boys were anxious to reach their destination. Except for a very brief meeting at Christmas, they hadn't seen Janet and Ann for a year. When the coach drew up in the main square of the little seaside town just before five o'clock, they were glad to alight.

Janet and Ann were waiting for them. They had happy faces.

'Hello, again,' they said.

Peter and John smiled broadly as they exchanged greetings. It was obvious the girls had changed very little, except that they had grown, like themselves.

'Thanks for the invitation,' John said simply, after they had retrieved their cases from the back of the coach.

'How are your parents and your grandfather?' Janet asked.

Peter smiled.

'Very well, thank you,' he said. 'And enjoying some peace and quietness now we have come down here! Do your uncle and aunt know what they are letting themselves in for, asking us to spend a fortnight with them?'

'We have given them good reports of you,' Ann laughed. 'We have told them you are as well behaved as ourselves!'

It was good to be with the attractive twins again. Janet and Ann were fine company, full of fun but sincere.

'Uncle's house is about a mile outside the town,' Ann explained. 'The bus station is around the corner. We shall be in time to catch the bus if we hurry.'

They just caught it. As the bus climbed slowly out of town in a low gear they had a glimpse of the harbour from their vantage point. The bus levelled off on the cliff top and they watched the sea, but a heat haze prevented them from seeing very far. A short drive brought them to the house.

'There it is,' Janet said, pointing across a meadow where a solitary pony pulled at the grass.

'I didn't realise it would be such a modern house,' Peter said. 'Look at the lovely big windows.'

'It's called *Sea Breezes*,' Ann replied. 'But you know that, of course.'

'It is well named anyhow, although there isn't any breeze today.'

Peter, licking his lips, could taste the tang of salt which was beginning to form on his face.

'Come along in, then!'

Somebody called across the meadow.

'There is Uncle at the gate,' Ann laughed. 'He wants to meet you.'

They hurried across the road and through the meadow.

'Welcome to *Sea Breezes*,' Mr. Mortimer said, extending his hand. 'Now, tell me. Who is who?'

'This is Peter and this is John,' Janet explained.

'Double trouble! With two sets of twins around we may expect some fun. Come along into the house,' he said.

They crossed a small patio where bright red geraniums bloomed. A fountain sent twin jets high into the air. Inside the house, the air conditioning kept the temperature even.

Mrs. Mortimer welcomed them warmly and suggested that the girls show Peter and John to their room while she busied herself with the finishing touches to the meal.

'Ready to eat in five minutes,' she said.

The meal was a very informal affair. The room resounded with happy chatter and Mrs. Mortimer made sure that they all had plenty to eat.

'Thank you so much for the meal. It was marvellous!' John said gratefully, when they had finished.

'Yes, rather!' Peter echoed.

Mr. Mortimer laughed.

'Food may have to be rationed on the island,' he warned.

'So we must eat as much as possible tomorrow,' Janet said.

They all laughed together.

'I can hardly wait to see the island,' Peter sighed. 'I wish the mist would clear for a few minutes.'

'Yes. It is rather a pity about the mist, isn't it? However, I can show you a plan of the island while my nieces are washing up. Would you care to come upstairs?'

The girls grimaced good-naturedly at their uncle.

'When we are on the island, we shall share all the domestic chores,' Ann said.

Mr. Mortimer's office was superb. It was the largest room in the house. A huge window, stretching right across one end, gave an uninterrupted view of the sea. The walls were decorated in black and white and all the furniture and equipment was white also. A wall-to-wall carpet provided the only colour. Peter pressed his toes deep into the luxurious orange pile.

'It's a wonderful room,' Peter said. 'Did you design it yourself?'

'I did,' Mr. Mortimer admitted. 'And the rest of the house, too. I'm glad you like it.'

They walked over to the other end of the room. A large white desk stood by a drawing board which had other equipment attached to it.

'This is my working area,' Mr. Mortimer explained. 'I am an architect and I do most of my work here.'

The architect took a large folder from a drawer and put the plan of his island on the board. Peter wondered how the paper stayed upright and then noticed the magnetic strip at the top of the drawing board. Similar strips were around the edge of the plan.

'If I had wanted to design an island, this is exactly how I should have planned it,' Mr. Mortimer said. 'We loved Shell Island as soon as we saw it, four years ago.'

Just at that moment the girls came in.

'Washing-up finished, sir!' Janet said, giving a smart salute. 'And nothing broken!'

'You were quicker than usual,' Mr. Mortimer observed.

'We wanted to help you tell the boys about the island,' Ann explained. 'Besides,' she protested, 'we are always quick with the chores!'

B

'I don't think I have forgotten what the island looks like,' the architect reminded his niece. 'But you two have spent more time over there than you have spent here this holiday. You might be able to refresh my memory. But remember—normally, this is a man's domain.'

Mr. Mortimer's eyes twinkled as he spoke.

'My great-uncle named the island because of the many tiny shells which litter the beach,' the architect continued. 'It was called by a different name before his time; indeed, I understand the name of the island has changed often over the centuries. My great-uncle died four years ago and left his island to me. I was his only relative.'

'You must have been delighted!' John exclaimed. 'Fancy inheriting an island!'

'It was a complete surprise. I knew nothing of the island until after my great-uncle's death. When I came down here for the first time I fell in love with it at once.'

'So you built this wonderful house,' Peter said.

'And when there isn't a beastly sea mist, you can see the island ever so clearly,' Janet said, peering out of the window. 'It is only about three miles out to sea.'

They all gathered round the plan again.

'The island is three quarters of a mile long and about half a mile broad, although it tapers a little at each end. The highest part of the island is to the north, facing us here. The ground rises to a hundred and fifty feet and slopes away quite steeply to the rocks below. It isn't dangerous if you take care.'

'The bay is on the south side of the island,' Ann continued, with her uncle's permission. 'This is the old stone jetty where we land.'

'And here, at the other end of the bay, is the old lighthouse,' Janet said, pointing on the plan. 'And, in between, a full half mile of golden sands.'

'You make it sound like a paradise,' Peter said wistfully. 'But how do we get there?'

'I keep a vessel in the harbour,' the architect explained. 'Her name is *Mariner*. She is nineteen feet long.'

'We shall introduce her to you tomorrow,' Ann said. 'There is quite a lot of rearranging of stores to be done before we go on the island.'

'We sail at three o'clock,' Mr. Mortimer said. 'And with all the gear aboard, we may have to make two trips. The girls seem to have collected enough equipment for a whole regiment!'

John smiled.

'It isn't everybody who has the chance to stay on a private island, is it?'

'Just like Robinson Crusoe,' Peter added.

'Oh, no! I don't want to meet any natives there!' Janet laughed. 'No footprints in the sand!'

Before going to bed they went for a walk along the cliffs. They strained their eyes to catch a glimpse of Shell Island but the mist had thickened. The little they could see of the water below them looked grey and lifeless, like the water left in the bowl after all the dishes have been washed.

'It isn't any use,' Ann said. 'We may as well have an early night and be refreshed for tomorrow. I expect the morning will dawn bright and clear and we shall be able to see the island easily.'

And she was right!

CHAPTER 3

Peter awoke first next morning. He glanced at his brother, who was still asleep. Then he flung back the covers and ran lightly across to the window.

The sea was very pale, reflecting the soft light of early morning. But the island was there—a shadowy shape out to sea, unreal, and seeming to float between sea and sky. Peter looked at his watch. It was just after four o'clock. No wonder everything looked dreamy!

He decided to climb back into bed and, very soon, he fell asleep again. He dreamed about the island. He was in a boat by himself, rowing as hard as he could. Yet he couldn't make any progress towards the indefinite shape which seemed to move further and further away from him. And then, just as he was giving up all hope of ever reaching his goal, something grabbed him by the shoulder and shook him. Slowly, he unscrewed his eyes. John was grinning down at him.

'Come and look at the island,' he said.

Slowly, Peter got out of bed and stumbled across to the window.

'Doesn't it look close!' John exclaimed.

Peter nodded.

'It does now,' he said, pinching himself to make sure he was really awake.

The sea had assumed the colour of the sky. It was bright blue with little flecks of white upon it where the tops of the waves twisted towards the shore. The early sun, slanting on the cliffs which made up the north side of the island, made patterns of alternate light and shade where the deep clefts bit into the rock.

John gave a great, long sigh of satisfaction. Peter blinked away his tiredness and stretched his long arms towards the ceiling. Then he began to dress himself.

'It looks exactly as I hoped it would,' he said, pulling his shirt over his head.

John was already dressed.

'I'll write a few lines to Mum and Dad while you are washing,' he suggested. 'There won't be a postbox on the island. We must write before we set sail. It was jolly decent of them to let us come here straight away.'

'Yes. It was,' Peter agreed.

He met Janet on the landing.

'Hello,' she said, brightly. 'Ready for breakfast?'

'I am!' Peter exclaimed, opening the bathroom door.

'You may have to cook it yourself, tomorrow!'

Peter chuckled to himself. He wondered what the girls and Mr. and Mrs. Mortimer would think of his cooking. He hadn't had very much practice. Neither had John. He hoped the girls wouldn't expect too much of them. After all, everybody had to learn.

By the time Peter had finished washing, John's letter was written and Peter's bed was made. The room looked very tidy.

'Thanks, John,' he said. 'Shall we go down now? I think breakfast is ready.'

They had another quick look at the sea to make sure the island hadn't floated away. Then they walked downstairs—quietly!

Mrs. Mortimer had cooked bacon and eggs for them.

'Hello, Peter. Hello, John,' she said. 'Would you mind banging the gong? Then my sleepy husband will come down, too. I trust you slept as well as he.'

'Yes, thanks,' John said. 'Is there anything we can do to help?'

Mrs. Mortimer shook her head.

'Nothing, thank you,' she replied. 'Janet and Ann were up with the larks. Everything was organised in next to no time! They are keen to show you over the island. If they had their way I believe we should have been there already!'

The boys laughed and Peter gave the gong a bang.

'All right, I'm coming!' Mr. Mortimer called as he flew down the stairs. 'I'm never late for breakfast.'

The girls gave him a disbelieving look.

'Well, hardly ever!' he added, smiling.

The sunlight flooded the breakfast room and they felt the warmth of it, gratefully. The day promised to be an excellent one, the breakfast was magnificent and the friendship enjoyed by all was very real. This was a happy home.

As Mr. Mortimer had a business appointment, he was unable to take the young people into town after breakfast. They wanted to check over the equipment on the boat in the harbour and he said he would join them as soon as he was free. The bus was due in a few minutes so they left immediately.

The harbour was a fascinating place. The tide was in and the small boats rode at anchor, moving gently as the water slapped their sides. *Mariner* was a red cabin cruiser and one of the largest in the quaint harbour. They rowed out to it in a dinghy and climbed aboard.

Peter and John stood unsteadily on the deck while Ann unlocked the cabin door.

The cabin seated five, but most of the spare room was filled with the stores the girls had gathered together over the course of the last few days. Needless to say, a large proportion of the cardboard cartons contained tins of food.

'It looks as if we are going to live on baked beans and soup!' John said, looking into one of the parcels.

Ann laughed.

'We've been very busy,' she said. 'We had to row all of these out here. But it has been good fun.'

'Shall we check the list to make sure we haven't forgotten anything?' Janet suggested. 'We don't want to leave anything behind, do we?'

So, getting in each others way, they attempted to find all the items which Janet checked off on the long list. It was a pleasant task and helped to add to the air of excitement all of them felt. By the time they had finished, half the morning had passed and they heard Mr. Mortimer hailing them from the harbour wall.

'I'll take the dinghy,' Peter said. 'I think I can manage it.'

He lowered himself carefully into the small boat and, taking up the oars, rowed the short distance across the harbour. Mr. Mortimer scrambled down the steps and Peter held the boat steady while he stepped aboard. Then, deftly, he swung the dinghy round and headed out for *Mariner*.

'Pipe the captain aboard,' Ann said, as she helped her uncle up on to the deck.

'Is everything shipshape?' he asked.

Janet peered out of the cabin.

'Oh, Uncle! Do you have to come in?' she said.

Mr. Mortimer laughed.

'We are not going to starve, at any rate,' he said. 'No! Perhaps I won't come in the cabin just now,' he agreed. 'Not until you have stowed some of those cartons into the lockers!'

So they set to work and made the cabin look much tidier. When they had finished they were quite pleased with it.

'Now you can come in,' Janet said.

Mr. Mortimer bent his back and scrambled down. He put two packages on the table.

'These will be good fun and useful, too,' he said.

The girls unwrapped the parcels.

'Walkie-talkie sets!' Janet exclaimed. 'We shall be able to keep in contact when we are on different parts of the island.'

They watched carefully as the architect showed them how to operate the sets, and they took turns until they were expert.

'These will be great fun,' Ann said, when they were packing the sets away again. 'What a wonderful idea!'

The architect smiled.

'Now back to the shore, into my car and away to the house,' he said. 'We sail at three o'clock this afternoon.'

John had a turn at the oars, and, after he had rowed the girls ashore, he went back for Peter and Mr. Mortimer.

The street by the harbour was crowded with holiday-makers watching the activities of the harbour people. The harbour was an interesting place and the many-coloured sails made a pretty picture. They threaded their way through the throng to the car park. Soon they were climbing the hill out of the town to *Sea Breezes*. Mrs. Mortimer had the meal all ready for them.

After lunch, Peter and John selected their most suitable clothes for their stay on the island, and then, squeezing into the car, they all drove down to the harbour and ferried themselves out to the cruiser. When they were safely aboard, Ann secured the dinghy on a short rope and they prepared to up anchor and sail away through the protecting harbour arms to the open sea.

John could hardly contain his excitement as Mr. Mortimer started the engine and they glided away through the water.

'Shell Island, here we come!' Mrs. Mortimer said.

Once clear of the harbour, the cruiser met the unprotected sea which tossed the boat up and down. Mr. Mortimer increased the engine's power to meet the surging water and, looking out of the portholes, the twins saw that they were making good progress towards the island.

'Doesn't the island look low in the water?' Peter said.

'That's because we are at sea level,' Ann laughed. 'When we look at it from the house, we are nearly level with the summit.'

The gulls circling round and round the cruiser seemed to lead them on to the island. It was probably the birds' home. The children waved to a pleasure-boat full of holiday-makers, and Mr. Mortimer altered course slightly to give the larger vessel a wider berth. Soon, they could pick out the details of the cliffs easily and Peter noticed that not all the cliffs were the same colour.

'This is where we alter course again,' Janet said.

They swung round to the west of the island to keep well clear of the rocks which jutted out for fifty yards or so from the base of the cliff. They were under the lee of the island now and the water was calmer. Then, rounding the western tip they met the full force of the sea.

'Nothing between here and France,' Ann said, bracing herself against the spray.

'We are nearly there now,' Mr. Mortimer smiled. 'Soon you will see the beach and the little stone jetty.'

'There it is,' Janet cried almost at once. She pointed through the cockpit door.

'Doesn't it look terrific!' John said.

They shaded their eyes from the sun and peered out across the water. The long strip of golden sand curved gently away to the south-eastern point of the island. Here the water was calmer and the waves seemed to lap the beach lazily, as though tired after their long journey. Above the beach the green vegetation climbed the hill and Peter spotted a cottage half hidden in the trees.

'What a beautiful little island!' he exclaimed.

With practised skill Mr. Mortimer brought the little vessel alongside the stone jetty with scarcely a bump. Janet and Ann leapt nimbly ashore and secured the cruiser fore and aft. Then they helped Mrs. Mortimer off the boat.

Mr. Mortimer had agreed to allow the young people to unload all the stores themselves, not that he was at all unwilling to do the bulk of the work himself but because he thought his nieces and their two friends would enjoy the task, hard though it would be.

'We'll get along up to the cottage then, dear,' he said to his wife. 'The crew will see to everything down here.'

Mrs. Mortimer smiled.

'By the time you have moved all this equipment you will be ready to eat again,' she said. 'It might be a good idea to move the food first.'

Peter laughed.

'Yes, ma'am,' he said, saluting. 'Just leave it to us and enjoy your holiday!'

Laughing, Mr. Mortimer took his wife's hand and walked along the jetty to the shore.

Peter and John went back into the cabin and began to lift out the heavy cartons on to the deck. When this was done, John jumped ashore and helped the girls stack them on the jetty as Peter passed the cartons across one by one. By the time they had finished, there was a large stack on the jetty, and Ann remarked that it looked something like the storeroom of a supermarket.

'And we made two trips over yesterday,' Janet said. 'The other things are in the cottage.'

Peter wiped his brow with his handkerchief and paused to survey the island.

'It's a marvellous place, isn't it?' he said.

'We think it's the best place in the world,' Janet replied. 'And we are glad to share it with you.'

'Yes. Welcome to Shell Island,' Ann said.

Peter and John looked into the girls' smiling faces.

'Thanks for inviting us,' John said simply.

CHAPTER 4

They dragged the cartons along the jetty and left them in a heap by the beach. The strip of sand was about fifty yards wide. There were thousands of tiny shells.

Janet surveyed the pile with satisfaction.

'This load would have been heavy for us to carry, wouldn't it?' she said.

'It's a good job we have the sledge,' Ann replied.

The boys looked curious.

'Come on,' she continued. 'We will show you where we hide the sledge and how we pull the things up to the cottage, too.'

They ran lightly across the soft, yielding sands to the foot of the cottage, which was built about thirty feet above the shore.

Janet groped in the undergrowth and pulled on a handle which poked through the bushes.

'Here it is,' she said proudly. 'This was our idea!'

'We were reading a book about Pitcairn Island in the Pacific,' Ann explained. 'The hills are very steep on Pitcairn, and the inhabitants use barrows like sledges to transport their produce from the hills to the boats on the shore. If the sledges run too quickly, the driver has only to lower the handles and two wooden runners dig deep into the sand at the back and slow the sledge down.'

They dragged the sledge across the beach quite easily and loaded the first batch of stores.

'Now pull hard!' Ann cried. 'We will have the things up to the cottage in no time.'

But it wasn't quite so easy as the girls had suggested, and John wondered how they were going to drag the vehicle up the steep slope to the cottage door. But the girls had a first-rate answer to this.

The largest tree on the island grew straight up from near beach level to beyond the little stone wall which marked the boundary of the cottage garden. Janet released a stout rope which was securely tied round two big hooks in the trunk and allowed the rope to slide slowly through her hands. Glancing up, they saw a little platform coming slowly down towards them.

'That's a wonderful contraption!' Peter exclaimed, full of admiration. 'I suppose you have fixed a big pulley in the higher branches.'

'Yes,' Janet replied. 'But this was Uncle's idea, not ours.'

The platform was secured at each corner by a rope fixed through a steel hoop. In fact, the platform itself was made of steel and it looked very strong.

'Would it support me?' John asked, liking the idea of a ride up through the branches.

'Oh yes, quite easily,' Ann replied. 'But we promised Uncle we wouldn't ride on it unless he was down here with us. He said we must be very careful when we use it for transporting the stores. It would give us quite a headache if it fell on top of us!'

The boys pulled steadily on the rope while Janet and Ann scrambled up the bank to the cottage. The girls made short work of unloading the cartons, and they left them in the garden before sliding down to where the boys stood. Then, dragging the sand sledge over the beach, they repeated the process five times. Within the space of an hour all the stores were at the cottage, the sledge was hidden away and the platform was secured high up in the tree.

The cottage was tiny, but picturesque. It had a real thatched roof and latticed windows which shone. The boys guessed that the girls had spent a lot of time cleaning them. Indeed, every part of the little house was spotless.

'Mind your heads,' Ann warned as they stepped over the threshold. The boys were tall for their age.

'We won't bring the boys in now,' Janet said to her aunt, who was busy in the kitchen which was very small. 'They can see everything in there when they do the washing up!'

They walked into another room which served as dining- and sitting-room combined. This room overlooked the beach. Glancing through the branches of the tree which hid the cottage partially from the sea, they saw the golden curve of the sand below. Beyond, the sea looked a deep blue. It would be difficult to imagine a better view. All was quiet and peaceful.

'Come on,' Janet said. 'We'll show you upstairs, if you can drag yourselves away!'

The stairs were narrow and access was gained through a door which Peter had imagined was a cupboard. He wondered how the Mortimers had managed to move the furniture upstairs, and then he guessed correctly that it had been hoisted through a first floor window.

Mr. Mortimer was on the tiny landing. He had a blue nylon tent in his arms.

'Can I help you?' Peter asked.

The architect shook his head.

'No thanks. We can put this up later this evening. There's plenty of time. I shall be glad of some assistance then.'

'It will be fun sleeping in a tent,' John said. 'We must remember to have our swimming trunks with us, in case we feel like a swim very early in the morning. It would be a pity to come into the cottage and wake everybody.'

Ann laughed.

'We plan to have some early swims, too,' she said. 'But come along now; we'll show you our room.'

The bedroom looked out towards the east where the old lighthouse was visible at the foot of the south-east tip of the island. The small, latticed windows were wide open and the pretty curtains flapped a little.

'The other bedroom has a much better view,' Janet admitted. 'In fact, the view is the same as from the dining-room except that one is higher up, of course, and one can see more of the beach. But I like this room best, myself.'

'Everything looks very comfortable, anyway,' John said, looking around. 'And I like your view of the old lighthouse very much.'

'And we see the sunrise in the morning,' Ann added.

'Tea is ready!' Mrs. Mortimer called from downstairs.

The table was placed right by the window. Looking down, they could see the full sweep of the bay from the jetty almost to the lighthouse which was hidden because the honeysuckle grew thickly around the left-hand side of the window. They were nearly through the meal when Peter noticed a small vessel rounding the headland.

'I wonder who that can be?' he asked.

Mr. Mortimer peered through the window.

'It looks like one of the fishing boats from the harbour,' he said. 'And it is coming in to the jetty.'

'You must go down and see what he wants, dear,' Mrs. Mortimer said.

'Yes, I must. Excuse me.'

They watched the architect scramble down the slope and walk across the beach to the black vessel which was just approaching the jetty. The fisherman threw a rope to Mr. Mortimer and the boat was secured. A few moments consultation followed and then the fishing boat slipped out to sea again with the fisherman at the helm.

'Nothing wrong, I hope,' Mrs. Mortimer said when her husband returned.

Mr. Mortimer looked rather worried.

'I hope not,' he replied. 'Apparently there is a telegram waiting to be collected at the post office. The messenger delivered it to the house but couldn't get any answer. He knows we keep the cruiser at the harbour and, as it wasn't there, he guessed we were over here. Hence the visit from the fisherman.'

'Oh dear. What are you going to do, then?' Janet asked.

'I'll have to slip across to the harbour. The telegram may contain a message from a client, but I wasn't expecting any urgent business. Anyway, the only way to find out is to collect it myself.'

'Perhaps Peter and John would go with you,' Mrs. Mortimer suggested. 'They will be able to row you to the shore and look after things on *Mariner*. It will save you having to anchor. That always takes time.'

'Would you mind?' Mr. Mortimer asked. 'It would be a help.'

'We'd love to come, of course!' Peter replied. 'Although I believe we were due to take a turn at the washing up.'

The girls volunteered to do it for them.

The wind had dropped somewhat and it was a perfect evening. The cruiser cut a white swathe through the water as they sped towards the harbour and, looking back, John was reminded of the vapour trails from high flying aircraft they saw sometimes in the blue sky. When they reached the harbour, Peter stayed on board while John and the architect lost no time in going ashore. The post office was just across the road.

Peter watched the other vessels while keeping an eye on the drift of his own. If *Mariner* started tossing in the wake of other cruisers his instructions were to drop the anchor. But the harbour waters, protected as they were, seemed calm. In next to no time Mr. Mortimer and John were back.

'It is bad news, I'm afraid,' the architect said. 'Mrs. Mortimer's father has been taken ill and we must go to him immediately.'

'Oh, I am sorry!' Peter exclaimed.

'I am wondering what to do about you young people,' Mr. Mortimer said. 'I am not too happy about leaving you on the island while we are away, but I know how disappointed you will all be if I have to take you off.'

The boys looked glum.

'We shall be all right on the island, really,' John said. 'And we will look after the girls, won't we, Peter?'

C

Mr. Mortimer smiled.

'Oh, yes, I know you will look after Janet and Ann,' he assured them. 'But what if there were some sudden emergency? Suppose one of you broke a leg? What would you do?'

'Couldn't we arrange with one of the fisherman to look in on us every day?' John asked. 'It may not be for long.'

'That is true,' the architect replied. 'We shall have to see how my wife's father is when we arrive. I expect Mrs. Mortimer will want to stay on there, in any case. It may be possible for me to return to the island in a couple of days. But, before we go back to Shell Island, I am going to telephone your parents and the girls' parents. They must give their permission.'

The boys' faces looked very sad.

'Oh, come now. I won't try to persuade them one way or the other,' the architect said. 'But I will point out that all the food is over there!'

'Thanks!'

Peter rowed Mr. Mortimer ashore, while John stayed aboard *Mariner*. He sat in the rowing boat by the harbour steps. For once, the time seemed to pass very slowly. At last, Mr. Mortimer returned.

'Back to *Mariner*,' he said, not giving any sign of the decision.

Peter rowed in silence. When they reached the cruiser, John was strangely quiet, too.

They climbed into the cockpit and secured the dinghy. Mr. Mortimer started the engine. It wasn't until they were clear of the harbour that Peter ventured to ask him the question.

'Can we stay, then?'

Mr. Mortimer looked at his anxious face.

'What's that you said?' he asked, teasing them.

'What did Mum and Dad say?' John asked.

The architect laughed.

'You can all stay!' he said. 'This will be a testing experience for you but I told your parents that I was sure they had made the right decision. And I have arranged with the fishermen to look in on you each day, as you, suggested.'

When they arrived back on the island, the happiness the boys felt at being permitted to stay was dulled by Mrs. Mortimer's anxiety about her father. Preparations for the Mortimers' departure were completed without delay, and it was a subdued group of young people that stood on the jetty waving a farewell as *Mariner* glided out towards the headland.

'I do hope everything will be all right,' Janet said. 'They have a long drive in front of them.'

When they got back to the cottage they decided to move all the stores which were still in the garden, but, in order to save space inside the cottage, Peter suggested they put all the tinned stuff under a tarpaulin. They agreed that this was a very good idea, and everything tinned was placed at the back of the cottage.

'This will be handy when it rains,' Ann remarked. 'We can reach anything near the top of the stack by leaning out of the kitchen window!'

But there was little prospect of rain. The complete absence of clouds indicated that tomorrow would be as pleasant as today.

'I know, let's prepare as much of the breakfast as we can this evening,' Ann suggested. 'And we can stock up with water, too.'

'Good idea. Then afterwards we can have a look at the lighthouse before going to bed.'

Peter was very keen to inspect the lighthouse.

So it was agreed that Janet and John should fetch the water while Ann and Peter stayed in the cottage to prepare for supper and lay the table for the morning. There was a fresh water spring on the island, which was delicious to drink. John grabbed a couple of polythene water carriers and followed Janet along the narrow path which wound away towards the western tip of the island. A light breeze was beginning to blow off the sea and Janet's long fair hair blew across her forehead. John thought what a pretty picture she made, walking along swinging a bucket carelessly. He wished he had a camera to capture the scene.

Soon the path widened and they walked side by side.

'How did the fresh water spring get on to the island?' he asked, marvelling at the gentle rippling noise he could hear in front of them.

'Uncle did explain to me a long time ago,' Janet replied. 'He said something about the water coming from deep, deep down inside the rock. After all, there is land at the bottom of the sea and the sea between here and the mainland is very shallow.'

'I suppose that is why the lighthouse was built years ago,' John suggested. 'It wouldn't do for any big ships to pass between the island and the coast, would it?'

They came to two very big rocks which lay back a little way off the path. The water bubbled out between them. John cupped some of the water in his palm. It was ice cold.

'It tastes marvellous!' he exclaimed.

Janet had brought a short length of polythene guttering with her. She placed this in the centre of the flow and the water ran down easily into the carriers. They soon collected sufficient for their immediate needs.

Later, they all took the path eastwards towards the old lighthouse, planning to have a closer look at it and at the causeway which joined it to the island at low tide. The sea had turned paler in the evening light. The waves were but small ripples, and John said the pattern of the sea reminded him of a huge sheet of corrugated cardboard spreading away as far as the eye could see.

The eastern part of the island was well wooded and they threaded their way through the trees until they were directly above the causeway.

'The path drops away here,' Ann warned.

They slid down the steep slope on to the soft sand. The lighthouse was about fifty yards away. The turning tide was lapping across the concrete walk.

'We won't be able to walk right up to the lighthouse this evening,' Janet said, looking at the sea.

The old structure was built of granite brought from Cornwall. It was about fifty feet high and it was built upon the rock formation which just appeared out of the water as each wave receded. Seven stone steps led up to a door which looked almost as solid as the rock itself.

'Does Mr. Mortimer own the lighthouse, too?' John asked. 'I should like to have a good look inside one day and to climb up to the top where the lantern is.'

'Oh, no,' Ann replied, shaking her head. 'I believe it is owned by the Trinity House people in London.

Didn't somebody come down to have a look at it two years ago, Janet? They had lunch with Uncle. Remember?'

'That's right. Uncle brought the man over here in *Mariner.*'

'I don't suppose the light would work after all these years, anyway,' Peter said regretfully. 'I wonder how long it is since it was used.'

But the girls didn't know.

They walked along the causeway as far as they could. The concrete was covered in green slime and it was very slippery.

'We shall be able to have a closer look in the morning,' John said.

They returned along the beach together in the failing light, climbing back to the cottage through the trees. Once in the cottage it was the work of a moment to connect the gas container to the cooker, and in a few minutes the aroma of baked beans and toast filled the kitchen. After supper, they tidied up and retired to bed. Until the Mortimers returned, the boys had been given the best room.

Neither Peter and John nor Janet and Ann needed any rocking to send them to sleep that first night on Shell Island. They were not to know then that other nights would be rather more eventful than this one. But, for the present, they were alone.

CHAPTER 5

Peter and John awoke early next morning to the sound of the song birds and the sea.

The sea looked very inviting and the broad strip of golden sand was too good to ignore.

'Shall we creep out and have a run on the beach before breakfast?' John asked, turning from the window.

'Rather!' Peter replied. 'But what about Janet and Ann?'

'There doesn't seem to be any sound from their room,' John said. 'I vote we leave them to sleep on. I expect they were very tired last night.'

Peter nodded.

'So was I,' he said. 'I slept like a log!'

They dressed in their bathing trunks and long-sleeved pullovers. It was only six o'clock, and the sun was weak, as yet. Closing the door quietly after them, they tiptoed down the narrow stairs. Peter was placing his feet carefully and he forgot about the low door at the foot of the stairs. He cracked his head on the lintel, and, rubbing his head vigorously, he bent almost double the rest of the way.

John couldn't help smiling.

'This is a little different from our normal rush down the stairs,' he said.

They slid down to the beach and ran across towards the sea. Two familiar figures were right at the other end of the sands by the causeway.

'No wonder we couldn't hear them in the cottage,' Peter said.

John shaded his eyes from the pale sun which was peeping around the cliff near the lighthouse.

'Halloo,' he cried, cupping his hands to his mouth.

The sound rang clear in the thin air of early morning. Immediately, the girls looked up and waved.

'Come on,' Peter said.

They raced across the firm sand by the edge of the water. Glancing back, John saw his footprints in the sand, and he began a long, weaving run, throwing up little clods of sand with his flying heels. He let Peter race ahead. He felt happy and free and he liked the way his feet marked the untrodden sand. It was as if this was his private island and he was treading where no other person had been.

'Hello,' he said, reaching the others at last. 'This is the life for me!'

Then, sensing that something was wrong, he spoke again.

'What have you two discovered now?' he asked.

Janet laughed uneasily.

'It looks as if we four have a mystery to solve,' she said.

'What do you mean?' John asked.

The girls pointed at the sand.

'Look at these,' Ann said.

John laughed.

'Oh, what big feet you have!' he exclaimed.

Janet tossed her head impatiently.

'Silly!' she said. 'These footprints were here when we came on to the beach this morning.'

'Wellingtons,' Peter said.

'Or seaboots.'

Ann had hit upon the truth.

'But who would want to land on the island?' exclaimed John.

'And are they still here?' Janet whispered.

John looked around cautiously.

'There doesn't seem to be anybody,' he said. 'But there must be twenty good hiding places on the island.'

They followed the trail of footprints to the causeway. It was obvious that whoever had landed had walked backwards and forwards between the causeway and the sea.

'It is fairly easy to calculate when he was here, anyway,' said John. 'The tide is still going out and these prints finish about twenty five feet from the edge of the water.'

Ann looked thoughtful.

'Good for you, John,' she said. 'I hadn't thought of that.'

'Well, how long would it take the tide to recede that distance?' Peter asked.

They all thought for a moment.

'I know. Let's all have a guess and then we'll take the average time and that should be near enough.'

They each measured up the distance in strides and then wrote a figure in the sand. Strange to say, they came to the same answer.

'Two hours. And it's nearly half past six,' Janet said.

'What was the time when you left the cottage?' Ann asked.

'Nearly half an hour ago.' John confirmed the time by his watch.

'And I ran round the bay right on the edge of the

water,' Peter said. 'I remember kicking up the spray with my feet.'

They ran back across the beach. Peter's footprints were still visible in the clinging, wet sand. The sea was about six feet away.

'So we were right,' John said. 'Somebody was here early this morning.'

They walked back up the slope to the cottage door, keeping their eyes open in case they spotted anybody in the trees. Everything seemed peaceful enough and in order. But they couldn't forget that the island had received an unknown visitor while they had been asleep in their beds.

'Shall we tell the fishermen?' Janet asked, over the breakfast table.

Ann was undecided.

'I don't know if we ought to or not,' she replied. 'What do you boys think?'

'I shouldn't tell them if I were you,' John said. 'They might telephone your uncle. He has quite enough to worry him at the moment, hasn't he?'

'And he may decide to rush back here,' Peter suggested.

'Oh dear. I hadn't thought of that,' said Ann. 'And, besides, we don't know anything about our visitor. He may have been a yachtsman who wanted to have a closer look at the lighthouse.'

'He wasn't driven ashore, that's certain!' Janet exclaimed. 'Look at the sea. It's as calm as a mill-pond!'

'I vote we don't mention it,' Peter said.

'Hear, hear!'

Everybody was in agreement. And they made up their minds not to let the strange incident spoil their holiday in any way. All the same, they would keep a careful watch in future.

After breakfast, Janet and John went to fetch the water, while the others cleared away the breakfast things. They had eaten well and it was clear that, with appetites sharpened by the sea air, there wouldn't be very much left in their larder by the end of the holiday.

At nine o'clock Peter and Ann ran down to the jetty to tell the fisherman, who had sailed into the bay to see if they needed anything, that all was well. By the time they returned, Janet, assisted by John, had completed the preparation of the vegetables for dinner. They were free to enjoy the morning as they wished.

'What are we going to do this morning?' John asked. 'Have you any ideas?'

'We'll do what you want to do,' Ann suggested. 'Then this afternoon we can enjoy ourselves on the beach when the sea has had a chance to warm up.'

'That will be excellent,' John agreed. 'The water felt rather chilly this morning. Can we explore the island now? Let's split up into twos. That way we shall cover more ground and we can keep our eyes open for any further signs of visitors.'

'Jolly good idea!' Peter said. 'You go east with Janet. Ann and I will explore the western side.'

'Lunch will be at one o'clock,' Janet said. 'First two back can put the vegetables on and lay the table!'

'Shall we take the walkie-talkie sets?' Ann said.

'That's a good idea,' Peter replied. 'They will be jolly useful, especially if we find something interesting.'

'Or somebody,' said John.

'Ugh!' Ann shivered. 'I hope we don't!'

They took an apple each from the store and filled their water bottles from the remains of the fresh water.

'I hadn't realised how much water we use,' John said. 'I suppose we all take it for granted when we can just turn on a tap and it gushes out.'

'It just goes to prove what clean people we are!' Janet joked. 'Anyway, we are very fortunate in having a fresh supply at the spring. Come on, John! If I am to show you all the best places above the caves we ought to leave at once.'

'See you later, then,' said Peter. 'Ann and I will take a good look at the west part of the island. Don't forget to keep your eyes open for any clues!'

They turned on to the path in opposite directions and with a happy wave they went their separate ways.

'I don't suppose we shall discover anything,' Ann said. 'There weren't any footprints around the jetty, were there? All the mystery seems to be at the lighthouse.'

'Well, don't sound so disappointed,' Peter chided. 'We don't want to discover anything, do we? This is too nice an island to have any mystery about it. Besides, we have only been here for a day!'

They reached the spring and had another close look at the crystal clear water bubbling out. Peter followed the trickle of water down the slope and noticed a wide area of wet sand at the foot of the rocks. The vegetation here was very green. He climbed back. Ann was sitting on a rock.

'It's a pity all that water goes to waste,' he remarked.

They continued round the curve of the bay to the

top of the headland, walking carefully on the narrow ridge which sloped down steeply on either side of them. They lay down on the spindly grass and watched the activity in the harbour.

'It is always very windy up here,' Ann said, watching the grass swaying to and fro. 'I shouldn't like to be up here in a storm.'

Peter agreed.

'But this is a marvellous observation point,' he said.

They could see every vessel leaving or entering the harbour. Even the small yachts were visible because of the bright sails most of them sported on their masts. To the east, the whole length of the bay was spread at their feet, curving, like a sickle, to the other headland by the lighthouse.

'I wonder if the others have discovered anything yet?' Ann said.

But they hadn't.

Janet and John had ambled leisurely across to the eastern coast line, because they wanted to see whether they could find any gulls' nests. The tide had turned and, sitting as they were directly above the caves, they could hear the peculiar sucking sound of the sea flowing through the cavities.

'Have you ever been in the caves?' John asked, turning to Janet who was gathering a few wild flowers.

'Oh, no! Uncle says the currents around this part of the island are quite dangerous and all the local yachtsmen keep well clear.'

'I was just thinking,' John replied. 'The sea must be right underneath where I am sitting.'

Janet looked alarmed.

'In that case we'll move back a bit,' she said.

They had another look at the lighthouse from the beach and watched the water sliding off the causeway back to join the sea which was creeping slowly up the sands. Long strands of dark green and brown seaweed draped the side of the concrete structure. It was just a little smelly.

Janet shuddered.

'If there is anything mysterious happening, this is the most suitable place on the whole island,' she said.

Presently, they turned their backs on the sea.

'Let's climb right to the top of the ridge and eat our apples up there,' John suggested.

They found a sheltered spot from which they could see a long stretch of the mainland and many of the gullies and crevices which clawed the cliffs of the north side of the island.

'That house over there is *Sea Breezes*,' Janet said, pointing across the straits in a north westerly direction.

John followed her gaze.

'Doesn't it look close!' he exclaimed. 'And we are not directly opposite, either.'

'I wonder how my aunt and uncle are getting on,' Janet sighed. 'What a pity they had to leave the island so suddenly.'

'I do hope you aunt's father will be all right,' John said.

'So do I. I prayed so much last evening that all would be well.'

John looked at her, doubtfully.

'Do you believe in prayer, then?' he asked. 'I was too tired even to think straight last night.'

Janet laughed.

'I was tired, too,' she said. 'The morning is the best time to pray. But, yes, I do believe in God and that the Lord Jesus has saved me from my sins because I have put my whole trust in Him. I can talk to Him just as easily as I am talking to you now.'

John fell silent for a long time. They watched the sea.

'Does Ann believe the same as you?' he said at last, having finished his apple.

Janet's face clouded.

'She thinks I'm silly, John.'

John got up. He wandered backwards and forwards along the ridge, deep in thought. Janet sat still. Suddenly, he returned to her.

'I think it's jolly unkind of Ann to think you are silly!' he exclaimed. 'I expect she went to sleep straight away, like the rest of us last night.'

Janet nodded her head.

'She did! And who could blame her?' she replied. 'Do you think I'm silly, too?'

'No! Definitely not!' he exclaimed, trying to sound convincing. 'It must be nice to believe.'

Janet smiled as John pulled her to her feet.

'Don't think too badly of Ann,' she advised. 'At least she is honest with me.'

'And I am not,' John said quietly, to himself.

Janet gave no sign that she had heard.

They walked slowly and silently through the trees. Suddenly, John stopped in his tracks and drew Janet down to the safety of the bushes.

'Did you hear what I heard?' he whispered.

Janet swallowed hard.

'Yes. I heard a noise, too. I think somebody else is

near us.'

They crouched there for about ten minutes. Whoever had been near had heard them also and was lying low. But there wasn't a sound to be heard.

'We can't stay here for ever,' John said. 'I'll stand up and see what happens.'

Very slowly, he stood up and looked around. Somebody else was doing exactly the same not twenty yards away. Peter was looking as worried as John felt!

'It's Peter and Ann!' John said, pulling Janet out.

They ran across the grass. Peter was laughing uncontrollably.

'We really are very sorry if we gave you a fright,' Ann apologised. 'But we weren't sure who you were, either!'

They all had a good laugh and felt much better for it.

'We mustn't let our strange visitor spoil our own holiday,' John said. 'But we thought you would be on the other side of the island.'

'We were. But we felt so hungry!' Peter said.

'So we called in at the cottage on the way back and put the vegetables on to cook. Then we came over here to find you,' Ann said.

'What is the time, then?' Janet asked, surprised that it would be so near to lunch-time.

'A quarter to twelve.'

John laughed.

'Some people seem to be permanently hungry,' he remarked.

After lunch, they wasted no time in getting down to the beach. It was a beautiful afternoon. The sun had warmed the sand and the water well. Both sea and sun bathing were a delight. Quite quickly, all tension and disturbing ideas slipped from their minds as easily as the water ran off their backs. They regained the holiday mood as though nothing had happened on the beach that morning. The sunny day passed very quickly and, too soon for them all, it was evening, and the fiery sun reddened the waves as it sunk into the horizon. Slowly, in the half light, they collected their things and returned to the cottage.

'It's all so peaceful,' Ann sighed.

'As though we were in a world of our own,' Peter said.

D

CHAPTER 6

Next morning, very early again, Peter and John crept down to the beach. For once, the girls were still in bed.

Long strands of seaweed were dotted here and there, showing how far the tide had smoothed the beach during the hours of darkness. By the water's edge the damp sand clung between their toes like rich brown sugar.

'I know now how Robinson Crusoe felt,' Peter said, as they ran towards the causeway.

'Peter's private island,' John laughed.

'Not quite,' Peter replied. 'But at least we haven't had any visitors during the night.'

The sand was quite undisturbed as far as they could see. About thirty yards away the silver sea swirled lazily around the rocks at the foot of the old lighthouse. It seemed as if the water was just awakening to the new day.

They climbed up to the causeway and walked along it. A crab scurried along from under their feet and clung precariously to the weed-draped edge. John lifted the little creature, taking care not to get in the way of its claws. He carried it along until he saw a pool and dropped the crab gently into the water.

'It's tall, isn't it?' Peter said, leaning back and looking directly up the side of the lighthouse.

John thumped the door with his fist.

'Solid too!' he said, rubbing his hand. 'This was built soundly!'

And this was true. The lighthouse was designed to keep out the sea, which, in the winter and sometimes at other times of the year as well, hurled itself on to the smooth walls of the old building. It had withstood the storms for over a century and had not yielded.

'I rather like this lighthouse,' Peter said. 'It isn't very beautiful but it has a special appeal of its own, I think.'

'Character?' John suggested.

'That's it. Character. It was always here when it was needed, warning the ships to keep well clear of danger and pointing the way to safety. I am sure the sailors were pleased to see the beam, especially when they were having a difficult passage.'

'I should like to go inside,' John said. 'I wonder if Mr. Mortimer has a key.'

'We could ask him when he returns, I suppose,' Peter replied. 'But the lighthouse doesn't belong to him, even though it stands on his island. It would be great fun to climb to the top. I wonder what it's like inside?'

They walked right round the base of the lighthouse, taking great care not to lose their footing on the slippery rocks. When, at last, they returned to the cottage, breakfast was ready.

'We seem to live on baked beans,' Janet apologised, when they were all sitting around the table. 'But we brought a good supply and it would be a pity to waste them!'

John laughed.

'They give a solid start to the day,' he said. 'Anyway, what's wrong with them? I love them!'

After breakfast they lost no time in getting down to the beach. The girls had been busy while Peter and

John had been idly discussing the lighthouse. A picnic lunch was already prepared and packed into the wicker basket the Mortimers used for this purpose.

Most of the day was spent in the water and, when they tired of swimming around, they lazed on the beach and allowed the sun to dry their bodies. On the west side of the jetty they found numerous little pools between the rocks. Peter put his hand into one of them. The water was warm.

'Let's see how many little creatures we can collect,' Ann suggested. 'It will be interesting to watch their antics. The water is quite shallow and very clear. We shall see how the different creatures get on with each other.'

So they collected small crabs and starfish. Peter found a big jellyfish which he lifted carefully on to a piece of wood and dropped gently into the pool they had selected.

John and Janet went off shrimping with a net they had brought from the cottage, and in a very short while they had a dozen or more shrimps of various sizes. They tipped them all in the pool and sat down to watch.

'They don't seem to mind all being in the pool together like that,' John observed after a long period of silence.

'Perhaps they have all had their lunch, like us,' Ann replied, 'and now they want to go to sleep.'

It was that sort of afternoon. Yesterday's breeze had gone and the air seemed heavy and hot. Even the gulls had ceased to whirl around the headland and were floating listlessly on the surface of the sea. There was scarcely a ripple on the water, except where the cross-currents swirled around the foot of the cliffs which guarded each end of the bay. Very soon the young people were dozing on the sand, except John, who was so fascinated by the creatures in the warm pool that he lay face downwards peering intently into the water. They ate a late tea, and, as they wanted to retire fairly early, they didn't bother to eat much supper.

'I hope the air is more bracing tomorrow,' Ann said, as they prepared to go upstairs to bed. 'It's strange how quickly the weather changes, isn't it?'

Peter and John wished the girls goodnight and went into their own room. They had just settled down for the night when there came an urgent knocking on their door.

Peter raised himself up on one elbow.

'What is the matter?' he asked sleepily.

It was Ann who answered.

'Can you both get dressed as quickly as possible and come into our room? There's a light in the lighthouse!'

Some of the excitement in her voice communicated through the door to their own hearts.

'Wow!'

John jumped out of bed at the same time as his brother and, in next to no time, they scrambled into their jeans and pullovers. They rushed through the open door of the other bedroom where Janet and Ann were watching at the window.

'There!' Ann pointed with her finger at one of the lower windows which seemed to be faintly lit.

'It may be the reflection of the moon,' Janet said. 'It's not a very powerful light, is it?'

But John shook his head.

'No moon tonight,' he said.

'In any case, the moon doesn't flicker,' Ann replied. 'And when I looked out of the window first of all I am sure the light flickered. You know, just like a fire!'

They peered across at the lighthouse again. Darkness was closing in rapidly and the granite structure was just a vague shape across the bay. There was not a breath of wind anywhere. The coming of night made the mysterious light clearer.

'It is some sort of a light,' Peter said emphatically. 'Think we ought to investigate?'

'Oh, yes!'

Janet was the adventurous sort.

'We can easily take a closer look without being seen,' she continued.

Ann and Peter looked doubtful.

'We could,' Peter said, dubiously. 'Or do you think we ought to wait until morning?'

John shook his head again.

'I should never sleep,' he protested vigorously. 'Besides, whoever is in the lighthouse might have gone by then, and we should miss them.'

'And do we want to meet them?' Ann asked.

Janet shivered.

'No,' she admitted. 'No! We don't! But we ought to try to find out what is going on, at a safe distance, of course.'

Peter decided it.

'All right,' he said. 'That sounds like a sensible suggestion. They must have come by boat, in any case, and it will help if we can see what sort it is.'

'Yes,' John continued. 'And you girls know most of the boats in the harbour. It may have come from there.'

So they put on their plimsolls while they thought about smugglers and wreckers and boxes of gold and wondered who the mysterious visitors were and what the light was.

They worked out a plan of campaign. Ann and Peter would stay under cover on the hillside above the light. Janet and John would tread softly along the edge of the beach where the trees overshadowed the sand. It would be pitch black there without any moon. They would keep in touch by walkie-talkie, speaking softly into the set.

'I'm glad Uncle brought the other set,' Ann said. She felt more confident now that they had decided on a plan. 'We have a big advantage over whoever is down there. They won't dream that anybody is spying on them.'

They crept downstairs and out of the cottage into the darkness. The only sound was that made by the waves as they kissed the shore. The trees were motionless. The air was still heavy. The sea was calm.

'The night is waiting for something to happen,' Janet said.

'Shoosh!' Ann whispered. 'We must be ever so careful.'

'And don't use the walkie-talkie more than necessary,' Peter warned.

John gripped his brother's hand.

'All right,' he said. 'We shall be careful. Goodbye.'

He led Janet quietly down past the big tree to the beach. The sea seemed a long way away. They walked cautiously along the beach under the trees, never stepping out of the inky black shadows. Some coins jingled in John's pocket and Janet stopped.

'Wrap them in your handkerchief,' she suggested.

They crept along towards the end of the causeway, stopping just in the shadows as near as they dared to venture. The light, a soft glow in the darkness, was still visible. They stood together, quite still, holding hands, wondering.

It wasn't so easy for Peter and Ann. They had to walk with extra caution along the path which ran parallel with the bay, about fifty feet above the sands. Here and there, little twigs were scattered in their path, and once, when Ann trod on one, they thought all the world could hear it snap. But, after listening carefully, they heard no sudden rush or alarm.

Peter fingered the walkie-talkie set.

'I'd love to know what John is thinking,' he said under his breath.

Ann nodded. Peter could feel the warmth of her breath as she nestled close to him.

'I expect he is just a little scared, like us,' she replied.

They chose a spot where they could see as much of the lighthouse area as possible, although the night seemed particularly dark. It was difficult to see anything more than five yards away. But the shape of the lighthouse was silhouetted against the slightly lighter colour of the sea and the soft glow of the mysterious light was easy to see.

'I wonder what it can be,' Ann whispered.

They were crouching between the bushes which grew thickly on that part of the island.

'Probably it is some kind of oil lamp,' Peter replied.

They watched in silence.

'It seems to be tinged with pink,' Ann said presently. 'You know, like the lamps they put on the roads to warn motorists of any repairs at night time.'

'A hurricane-lamp, you mean.'

Ann nodded.

'I wonder how the others are getting on?' she whispered.

Janet and John were thinking the same thoughts on the beach. All was perfectly quiet. But for the strange light, nothing would seem to be amiss.

'Let's call up Peter and Ann,' Janet suggested. 'There doesn't seem to be any point in standing here just waiting for something to happen.'

John eased the set on to the beach and carefully extended the aerial. He switched on. With his lips resting on the mouthpiece, he spoke into it very softly.

'Hello,' he said. 'Can you see anything interesting up there?'

Peter jumped. John's voice sounded so near.

'No!' he breathed into his set. 'Only the light. Where are you, exactly?'

'Under the trees near the end of the causeway,' John said. 'Where are you?'

Ann took the set.

'About forty feet above your head,' she said, amused that they were so close. 'If we rolled a pebble down the hill it would land right at your feet!'

John grinned.

'Janet wants to speak to you,' he said.

He handed the set to Janet and sat down on the beach, listening to the sea and to Janet's quiet voice speaking to her sister. He felt rather fed up. They seemed to have got nowhere. He wanted to creep along the causeway to make a closer investigation of the old lighthouse, but he knew the others would not agree to this course of action. Obviously, someone was inside, or had been inside and left the lamp burning. It would be better to remain unseen. He chuckled to himself. It was a strange situation. Here they were, on an island, completely cut off from the other world of the mainland. What could they do, even if they discovered something important? They couldn't contact the authorities, even if they wanted to. Casually, he glanced across at the light. It wasn't there!

He grabbed the set from Janet.

'Peter! Ann!' he gasped. 'The light has disappeared!'

Janet looked across the beach and, instinctively, drew a little closer to her friend.

'What shall we do now?' she whispered, trying to keep her teeth from chattering. 'Oh, John, I'm scared!'

'Stay where you are,' John told his brother, over the set. 'And if you see anything, don't call me. Just keep very still. We may see some action in a moment!'

They strained their eyes to catch a glimpse of whoever might be close to them. John wished it had been a little lighter, for, although they were deep in the shadows and quite secure while they kept still, it was almost impossible to pick out any movement around the rocks. But they could hear. The stillness of the night amplified the very breath they drew. Suddenly, quite distinctly, they heard a noise. Somebody was opening the lighthouse door. From the inside!

It was a heavy door, yet it swung easily on its hinges and would have been perfectly silent, except for the rust which had attacked the metal. They heard a long creak. After this, for twenty seconds or so, there was quietness. Then they heard another creak and a dull thud as the door was closed carefully. The unseen watchers listened as though they were rooted to the spot on which they crouched. They heard the faint tinkling of keys. Then, footsteps!

It wasn't so bad for Peter and Ann. They were up among the bushes, like spectators watching a scene in an arena. They were out of harm's way. But Janet and John were on the beach. And Janet wanted to scream!

'He's walking along the causeway!' John whispered, gripping Janet's arm. 'He will pass very close to us, but, if we keep still, he won't see us.'

Janet stuck her handkerchief in her mouth and did as she was told.

They listened to the splash of the water which covered the far end of the causeway. The visitor wore rubber boots. They could hear the tops of them rubbing together as the stranger walked along. They had a brief glimpse of him as he turned towards them and came down the steps. He was stockily built, but they could not see clearly enough to be sure of his features. Then he walked towards the sea, his back towards them, unaware that he was being watched.

Janet and John breathed a sigh of relief. Janet opened her mouth to speak but John restrained her. Enthralled, he was trying to see what the man was doing. They listened for the tell-tale sound of oars, but heard nothing. The man had gone, like a wisp of smoke. He seemed to have walked out to sea. He had vanished in the night!

'Well!' John said. 'What do you think of that?'

Janet shivered again.

'I'm glad he has gone and I hope he never returns,'

she said. 'Let's speak to the others and ask them if they heard anything.'

Peter and Ann were very relieved to hear the voices over the set.

'Are you two all right?' Peter asked anxiously.

John reassured his brother.

'Yes,' he said. 'The stranger came very close, but he didn't see us. Did you see him?'

'No. But we think we saw the boat,' Peter replied. 'We also saw a light out to sea, like a yellow pinprick.'

'Good! I thought he must have helpers somewhere out there. Can you slide down here now, Peter? We can't do very much more tonight, can we?'

'No,' Peter agreed. 'Except go back to the cottage and get some sleep. It's after midnight!'

It was good to be together again.

'I vote we don't split up any more,' Ann said, when they were all on the beach. 'It was horrible being separated. And so dark.'

'Never mind,' John said. 'At least you saw a light out to sea. We couldn't have seen that from where we were. We only saw the vague shape of a man.'

Ann shivered.

'Ugh!' she said. 'Let's get back to the cottage straight away!'

CHAPTER 7

They slept well into the next morning. When finally they awoke it was with a feeling of refreshment and ease. The events of the night seemed but a dream.

Certainly the island looked peaceful enough. The skies had cleared and the sun had returned, making the sea look as though a million tiny stars had been scattered upon it. The birds had resumed their song long before the sleepers had roused from their slumber, and, in contrast to the night, all seemed activity.

Peter watched the bees going from blossom to blossom among the flowers which grew directly beneath the window.

'The bees make me feel quite lazy,' he said to his brother, who was dressing slowly.

'We are on holiday, though,' John reminded him. 'It is becoming quite exciting, isn't it?'

Peter smiled thoughtfully.

'We can have a close look at the lighthouse rocks after breakfast,' he suggested. 'We might find a small clue there.'

They went downstairs and busied themselves preparing the meal. They were almost ready to eat breakfast by the time the girls came down.

'Hello, sleepyheads!' John teased. 'Don't you know the time?'

Ann yawned and shook her head.

'No,' she replied. 'We forgot to wind our watches last night. It's about seven, isn't it?'

Peter laughed.

'It's nearly nine,' he said. 'Just after low tide.'

'It's funny how islanders take more notice of the tide than of the clock,' Janet observed. 'We are quite new to this sort of life, and yet, already, we time ourselves by the sea.'

'And the sun,' Ann added. 'We go to bed when the sun sinks into the sea.'

Peter gave her a disbelieving look, and Ann had to add to her statement.

'Or soon after,' she said.

Over breakfast, which they ate slowly, they discussed the events of the previous evening.

'I am quite sure there is something sinister about our visitor,' Ann said. 'What was he doing in the lighthouse all that time?'

'And how did he unlock the door?' Peter asked.

Janet shook her head.

'I don't know,' she admitted. 'But I would like to read something to you, if I may.'

'Go ahead,' Peter said.

She drew a Gospel of St. John from her apron. Peter looked very surprised.

'It is strange how often my daily reading is so suitable,' she continued. 'Last night we were out of our beds and in the darkness because somebody was where he had no right to be. Now, listen to this!'

She rested the little book on the toast rack and began to read.

'And this is the condemnation, that light is come into the world, and men loved darkness rather than light, because their deeds were evil. For every one that doeth evil hateth the light, neither cometh to the light, lest his deeds should be reproved.'

'They won't come back in the daytime,' John said, greatly impressed by what Janet had read. 'May I borrow your little book, Janet? I'd like to hear some more.'

Ann changed the subject quickly.

'So we shall enjoy our holiday again,' she said.

'And at night?' Peter asked, still wishing to talk about the previous evening.

'We solve the mystery of the island,' John replied.

Ann was more practical.

'Come along, now,' she said. 'We must clear away the breakfast things and then we can all go for our swim. Look how beautiful the sea is today! Let us make the most of every minute.'

They bustled around so much that, in the confined space, they bumped into each other frequently. Janet decided to create more room by giving the boys all the available water carriers and sending them off to the spring to fill them. By the time Peter and John returned, they had cleared up the little cottage and were ready to change into their beach clothes.

'This is silly!' John said, as he struggled into his bathing trunks. 'I vote we always dress for the water as soon as we get up, if it is a nice morning. We must ask the girls to do the same. We don't want to waste a minute.'

Indeed, every sunny moment was becoming more precious for they all believed that, when Mr. Mortimer returned, he would take them off the island. They would have to tell him about the stranger at the lighthouse.

The beach, as always, felt delightful. The sea had crept up the sand while they slept, washing each particle, purifying the whole, until an untrodden arc of smooth gold awaited their feet. They ran in and out of the water, criss-crossing the beach until their footprints seemed to be everywhere. Then, tired of chasing around, they lowered their glistening bodies into the warm sea and lay idly floating on the water, as the seagulls had done on the previous day.

Later, they swam across to the foot of the rocks where the lighthouse stood. Shaking the water from their bodies, they trod the slippery boulders on the seaward side of the old structure.

They examined the rusty links carefully. Then they looked for other clues but, apart from the chain, the rocks were bare. And slippery. Once Janet lost her balance. Only John's strong arm prevented her from sliding into the sea.

'That man must have been as agile as a cat!' Ann exclaimed. 'Fancy clambering over these rocks in the pitch darkness. It's bad enough now!'

'Do you think he will come back tonight?' Peter asked. 'If he does, we can easily untie his boat and let it drift away.'

Janet looked horrified.

'No thank you very much!' she exclaimed. 'We don't want him on the island with us, do we?'

Peter shook his head.

'I hadn't thought of that,' he admitted.

They walked round the lighthouse to the door, which looked as if it hadn't been opened for years. It was securely locked, of course. They hadn't expected otherwise. But they would have given anything to peep inside, just to see what was in there.

'We can easily tell if it is opened again,' John said. 'Even if we are asleep.'

'Oh, I know,' Ann interrupted. 'Put a piece of

cotton across the door and, if it is broken in the morning, we shall know somebody has been here.'

'Clever girl,' Peter said. 'But we haven't any cotton.'

'I can probably find some back at the cottage,' Janet suggested helpfully.

'That won't be necessary,' John said. 'We can use one of Janet's long hairs!'

In spite of loud protests and a scuffle on the causeway, they managed to hold Janet still for long enough to pull one of her fair hairs from her scalp. Then, laughing loudly, they all lent a hand in twisting the hair around two small protrusions at the bottom of the door, securing it carefully so that it could not be disturbed by the wind.

'You can't see it, even in the daytime,' Peter said, standing back a couple of yards. 'And it is above the reach of the sea.'

'Now let's forget it again,' Janet said gaily. 'Back to the water as fast as we can!'

They raced down the causeway and tore across the beach together. Four clouds of spray flew up from the water as their bodies hit the sea. It was a wonderful morning!

Peter turned to Ann, intending to remark upon the perfection of the day, when he noticed Janet and John, who had swum a little way off, returning at full speed.

'What is the matter with you two?' he asked, sensing that they were not just trying to race each other.

John shook the water from his eyes.

'We swam out until we were level with the headland,' John explained. 'There's a boat coming this

E

way, heading straight for the island. It doesn't look like an ordinary fishing boat.'

'Not *Mariner*!' Ann exclaimed. 'Not already, surely!'

Janet shook her head.

'It's a strange vessel,' she said. 'One that I haven't noticed in the harbour.'

'I thought it would be wise to keep out of sight,' John suggested. 'We don't want anybody to know we are here, especially if they are up to some mischief.'

'All right, then. Back to the beach, quick!'

Peter started to run for cover and, as they crossed the sands, he thought how silly it was to pretend nobody had been on the island. The beach was marked with their footprints everywhere.

They spread themselves among the bushes just in time to see a sleek, blue motor boat round the headland. They heard the hum of the engine and saw a lone man sitting behind the windscreen.

'He looks harmless enough,' John observed. 'I wonder if he knows we are watching.'

'I think we just reached cover in time,' Janet replied.

The man cut out the engine. The boat glided silently across the last few yards of water to the jetty. He threw a rope over one of the bollards and secured the stern. Then, unhurriedly, he climbed on to the rough concrete and started to walk towards the beach.

'Here he comes,' Ann whispered.

They watched as he examined the footprints in the sands. He seemed to smile. Then he cupped his hands to his mouth and called out. The sound of his voice rang through the clear air.

'Halloo . . .'

'What do we do now?' Janet asked.

'We had better go across to see what he wants,' John said.

Rather sheepishly, they got up. Fortunately, at that moment, the man turned his back towards them to look at his boat. They hurried out into the open. When he turned round, he saw them immediately.

'Oh, there you are,' he said, looking at their wet bodies. 'So you were hiding from me, were you?'

Ann blushed.

'We didn't know who you were,' she explained.

'And we still don't know,' John said, rather boldly.

The man looked at John, keenly.

'I hoped to receive a more friendly welcome,' he said.

John shifted his weight from one foot to the other. He felt very uneasy.

'I'm sorry,' he apologised. 'But who are you? And why have you come?'

The man's face relaxed into a smile.

'I'm from the post office,' he explained. 'Mr. Mortimer was on the telephone this morning and he asked me to come across to make sure you have everything you need. It was a good opportunity to try out my new boat.'

'It's a very nice one,' Ann said.

'Did my uncle say when he would be coming back?' Janet asked.

The man shook his head.

'He didn't say exactly,' he replied, 'but he hopes to return in a day or two, when your aunt's father is a little better.'

The man paused and looked around.

'Nice little hideaway you have here,' he said.

Janet agreed.

'You must come up to the cottage and have a good look over the island while you are here,' she said, rather belatedly. 'It was good of you to call in with my uncle's message.'

The man smiled.

'Thank you all the same,' he said, 'but I have my work to do. If there is anything you need, though, I'll see that you have it.'

The girls thought they had enough food to last them all until their uncle's return. There was a good supply of tinned food left and plenty of butter and eggs.

'We may be rather short of bread,' Ann said. 'We have eaten rather a lot since we came! But we can manage if it isn't convenient for you to call in again.'

'Oh, that's no bother. If you want bread you shall have it. And milk, too!'

'All right,' Janet smiled. 'Three pints, please. We brought some tinned milk with us, but it would be lovely to have some fresh milk for a change. Thank you very much indeed.'

They walked back along the jetty with the postman.

'I'm sorry we treated you like we did,' John apologised again. 'But we wondered who you were.'

'Think nothing of it,' he replied. 'You weren't expecting a visitor, were you? Anyway, you will know who it is this evening. I'll bring your shopping across at eight o'clock.'

They thanked him and helped him down into his boat. For the first time, Peter saw that the man wore low cut rubber boots. The others seemed not to have noticed.

'Goodbye,' the postman said as he thrust the boat away from the jetty, 'until this evening.'

They watched the small vessel slide through the water towards the headland. Peter made a mental note of the engine beat in case he heard it again, after dark. As he stood with the others, waving, he wondered. Could this friendly postman be their night visitor?

'Well, that's that!' Janet said, as they walked back to the cottage. 'I must say, I do feel rather silly.'

'So do I,' said Ann. 'Don't you think we are carrying this lighthouse business too far?'

Peter shook his head.

'We shall have to wait until tonight,' he replied.

The man returned at the appointed hour, bringing the provisions with him. The sea was much rougher. He gave the packages to the girls while Peter and John tried to steady the boat.

'Can you post these for us, please?' Peter asked, handing him the letters they had all written during the afternoon. 'We have put stamps on them.'

'Of course. You have given them to the right person,' he said.

'I'm sorry we can't pay you for the shopping,' Janet began to explain.

'That's quite all right,' the postman replied. 'Mr. Mortimer told me he would settle the account when he returned. We are good friends. You don't need any money on an island.'

'Thank you for all your kindness,' Janet said sincerely. 'The fresh milk will taste delicious and we shall have plenty of bread now.'

'Good. Then I'll be off home before this sea becomes even rougher. Mind you all go to bed early,' he said, with a twinkle in his eye. 'Goodbye.'

'I wonder why he said that?' John said, after the boat was out of sight.

'Perhaps Mr. Rubberboots wanted us to be asleep for a special reason,' Peter replied.

But the girls only laughed.

'I'm sure he isn't our strange visitor,' Janet said.

CHAPTER 8

They ate a wonderful supper that evening. The excitement of the day had in no way spoiled their appetites, and Janet, who usually did the bulk of the cooking, was kept busy supplying their needs. After supper they talked.

'But lots of sailors wear rubber boots!' Ann explained in answer to Peter's theory that their unexpected visitor might be interested in the lighthouse.

Peter sighed.

'Call it a hunch if you wish,' he said, 'but it seemed strange that he should mention about us going to bed early tonight.'

'Oh, I don't know,' Janet replied. 'Probably he didn't quite know what to say, so he said the first thing he thought of. He must have felt rather embarrassed by our strange behaviour.'

'But if the lighthouse is used by smugglers from a foreign country, they would have to have local contacts to distribute the stuff,' John said. 'Oh, I'd love to see inside!'

Ann laughed.

'Uncle will be back in a couple of days, I expect,' she said. 'We must tell him everything we know and then he can decide upon the right course of action. After all, it is his island!'

Peter nodded.

'I suppose so,' he said. 'But we ought to protect it

for him while he is away. I vote we have another look at the lighthouse tonight.'

'Hear, hear!'

John was willing for anything.

Janet and Ann sighed.

'We knew you would want to have another look tonight,' Ann said. 'And they say girls are curious!'

'We'll stay here, then,' Janet said. 'If you are not too long we shall have a hot drink waiting for you, when you return.'

'All right, then,' Peter agreed. 'And you can have the other walkie-talkie and we can tell you what we are doing.'

'That's right,' said John. 'You can time our return to a minute and our drink will be all ready for us before we tumble into bed!'

Janet yawned.

'Oh dear,' she said sleepily. 'Don't be too long, will you?'

Darkness was closing in when the boys left the cottage. The strong breeze ruffled the leaves of the big tree and all along the shore the waves smacked the sand. Once John thought he heard the sound of oars creaking in rowlocks but it was difficult to isolate any one sound from among the others. The wind set everything in motion.

'The lighthouse looks very black tonight,' Peter said, as they stood quietly in the shadows by the causeway. 'No sign of any light.'

'Shall we have a closer look, then?' John asked. 'It won't do any good, I suppose, but it will be fun walking along the causeway in the dark. I wonder if it is awash at the other end.'

Peter grinned.

'I don't know if the girls would approve,' he said, 'but I'm game. It won't do any harm, after all.'

'We won't talk, though,' said John, clutching the set tightly. 'Not until we get back to the beach.'

Silently, for their rubber plimsolls made no noise, they climbed the dozen steps which led to the top of the causeway. They walked along carefully. The concrete was slippery under foot and once John grasped his brother to prevent himself from falling. The lighthouse end of the causeway was awash. Peter winced as he felt the water creep up his legs.

'We should have taken off our socks,' he whispered to John.

They edged around to one side of the old lighthouse which loomed above them like an inky black cigar pointing into the sky. They were just about to return to the shore when, instinctively, they drew back. Quite clearly, they heard a sound. Somebody was inside!

Flattening themselves against the lighthouse wall they stood rooted to the spot. A wave swirled high up their legs and John thought how very soon they would have to return to the shore. But neither wanted to move away.

'Are you afraid?' Peter breathed into John's ear.

'No! Look, I'm going to get inside the lighthouse if I can. I've got the set and if I can hide myself in a dark corner I might be able to tell what is happening.'

Peter was appalled! He was about to tell his brother that he was to do nothing of the kind, when they heard another sound. The door creaked open slowly and somebody came out.

The stranger might have walked around their side of the lighthouse but, fortunately, he chose to walk the other way. They had a glimpse of his back and then, before Peter could restrain his brother, John leapt up the steps and darted through the open door.

A surge of anxiety came over Peter. But he dare not call out. The man, who had probably gone to make sure his boat was secure behind the lighthouse, would be back in a minute. Which way would he choose? Peter decided to stay where he was, hoping the stranger would return by the same route he had taken. This was a wise decision. As the man came back it was all Peter could do to restrain himself from crying out. John was inside. And the stranger was shutting the door!

Peter listened to the jingle of keys and then heard the man stride off along the causeway to the beach. He waited. There was a splashing sound from below and Peter guessed correctly that the man was wading out to his boat which must have been secured at the foot of the rocks. He strained his ears to catch every sound. The man grunted as he climbed into the boat and pulled against the incoming tide. Distinctly, for he was so near, Peter heard the rowlocks creak, and, peeping carefully around the lighthouse, he saw a vague shape sitting in the small boat rowing out to sea.

Another wave swamped Peter and he decided that he would have to return to the beach. John was safe in the lighthouse, locked in for the night, at least. The man had left the island. Even as Peter reasoned, he could hear the low hum of an engine. So that was it. The visitor had a motor boat moored in the bay!

Peter risked a quick bang on the lighthouse door but he guessed that John was up aloft somewhere.

The thick walls and doors were an effective barrier to any sound. Reluctantly, he decided his brother would have to spend the night in the dark. Alone. He hoped he wouldn't be afraid.

He walked along the causeway, holding on tight to the iron rail to support himself against the sea. He was glad when he reached the safety of the beach. Quickly running up to the cottage, he knocked on the door. Ann let him in.

'Where is John?' she asked. 'And look, Peter! You are wet through!'

Janet appeared at the door of the kitchen.

'You are a fine pair!' she chided, attending to the cocoa and not noticing Peter's condition. 'Why didn't you call us up on the set? We haven't heard a sound from you since you...'

She broke off abruptly, put the cups down and steadied herself.

'What has happened? Where is John?' she asked fearfully.

Peter quickly soothed her.

'Don't worry, Janet,' he said in a calm voice. 'John is safe inside the lighthouse and we can get through to him on the set.'

'How did he get inside?' Ann asked. 'Did the visitor come back?'

Peter nodded.

'Yes,' he said. 'We hid on the rocks and, when the man came out of the lighthouse to check on something, he left the door open. Before I could stop John, he darted inside. Then the man came back and locked the door.'

'Has the stranger gone now?'

Janet looked anxious.

'Oh, yes. He rowed out to sea and I heard the sound of an engine. He must have moored his boat about a quarter of a mile from the shore.'

'Here is your cocoa,' Janet said. 'Can you drink John's, too?'

Peter said he could.

'I hope John will be all right,' he continued, looking very worried. 'Fancy spending the night in that old lighthouse, alone!'

'We'll get the walkie-talkie set while you are having your warm drink and changing your trousers,' Ann suggested. 'And don't worry too much. John will be quite safe where he is and we can cheer him up no end.'

But there was no reply on the set, although they tried for an hour to make contact.

'He has fallen asleep,' Ann suggested.

'Or dropped his set and broken it,' said Janet.

But Peter wouldn't be consoled. He blamed himself for allowing his brother to go inside the lighthouse.

'We must be up at dawn,' he said. 'Somehow, we must get into that lighthouse!'

They went to their bedrooms to try to sleep, but, for once, sleep did not come easily, and, when finally they dozed off from sheer exhaustion, it was to dream about lighthouses and spiral staircases. Janet dreamed she was falling down into a bottomless pit and she awoke with a start, hoping that the dawn would be streaking the sky with long, red fingers. But no light appeared towards the east. Disappointed, she went back to sleep.

John's first thought as soon as he was inside the old

lighthouse was to find a place to hide. The man, who had left the door open, would surely return, and if he discovered John the effort of getting inside the lighthouse would have been wasted. Besides, the man would be very angry.

It was pitch dark inside, except for a faint tinge of grey around the door. As yet, John's eyes were unused to the intense blackness. He groped around trying to find the stairs which would lead him to the security of the upper floors. In order to have both hands free he left his walkie-talkie set under a pile of tarpaulins he discovered when he nearly fell headlong over them. But he couldn't find the stairs!

He wished Peter had come in with him. Two heads were better than one in a situation like this. And the man would soon return. Then, quite suddenly and very naturally, John decided to ask God for help. He didn't kneel on the floor. He didn't shut his eyes, even. He just spoke as if God were with him in the darkness, like a friend, as Janet had told him.

'Help me to find the stairs quickly,' he prayed. 'I must hide before the man comes back!'

Without intending to, he bowed his head as he shuffled along. When he straightened he felt a sudden blow. He winced and for a moment felt very sick. But his prayer was answered. The stairs were right above him. He had found them with his head! He slid his hands along the steps one by one from the underside until the space was so cramped that he knew he was at the bottom. Crawling out from underneath, he found the handrail and the right side of the stairs. Thankfully, still clutching his bruised head, he stumbled up the stairs. He had mounted only a dozen steps when he heard the man at the door.

John pressed himself against the wall and waited. There was no sound in the lighthouse at all. If the stranger had entered the lighthouse as quietly as he stood in the doorway now, John would never have heard him and he would have been caught. But, mercifully, the man was unaware of his presence and John breathed a great sigh of relief when he heard the keys in the door which closed with a clang. Once more, he was alone.

He waited a few minutes and retraced his steps down in order to collect the set. But it was difficult to find. He kept close to the wall and trod warily, with his hands outstretched in front of him. Several times his feet encountered tarpaulins and he felt under these carefully. By the time he had completed the circle and regained the foot of the stairs he was still empty-handed.

'I'll find it in the morning,' he said, half aloud.

The intense quietness was disturbing. It was a relief to hear his own voice.

He began to mount the stairs which were fixed in spiral fashion to the interior wall. The lighthouse was about twenty feet across and the steps seemed to climb upwards in a never-ending coil. John gripped the handrail, firmly. Soon there was a change in the pattern of steps and he edged off to his right for a yard or so. Reaching out, his hands felt a door and, discovering a handle, he turned it. To his delight the door opened.

'This must be a storeroom,' John said quietly. 'There should be a ladder leading up to the next floor.'

He didn't want to waste any time. His objective was the top, where he might obtain a glimmer of light from the sky, if not for an hour or two, certainly later on towards the dawn. The darkness was becoming unbearable.

He discovered the ladder quite easily. As he climbed it warily, he felt the cold, smooth metal in his hands. He was surprised at its smoothness. There was no rust on it and he guessed, rightly, that it was made of steel. When his feet were on the eleventh rung his head made gentle contact with a trap-door. It was locked.

'Oh dear! It would be!' he said.

He retraced his steps down to the floor and sat on what seemed to be a long coil of rope. It was disappointing to reach so far and not to gain the top. He felt in his pocket for his handkerchief and, in doing so, discovered the little torch he had placed there before leaving the cottage. It was a few minutes before he found enough courage to switch it on. The darkness, although unpleasant, prevented him from discovering fresh dangers. The tiny beam pierced the blackness. He swung the torch everywhere.

'It is a storeroom,' he said.

Everything was arranged neatly, as though the lighthouse men who once lived there were coming back with the dawn. Ropes were coiled neatly, lanterns were arranged on a shelf, though there was no oil in them, and various tools were in their allotted place around the wall. But John decided not to stay. He would have another look at the trap-door.

He discovered two heavy bolts on the door, and, pleased with himself, he quickly drew them back. Then, pushing with all his strength, he forced the door open, sliding it aside enough to scramble through into the room above.

He was glad of the torch. There was hardly room to move up there. Machinery for working the light was everywhere and it was spotlessly clean.

'I wonder if the light would work after all these years,' John said aloud.

He felt less fearful now he had reached this far. He knew that the ladder in the corner of this smaller room would lead him to the lantern. He would spend the rest of the night up there.

Greatly encouraged, he climbed the ladder and unbolted the door which swung up on two hinges. He eased himself through. It was lighter at the top, and very quiet.

CHAPTER 9

After the activity of the previous days it was good to sit still. In the tiny space at the top of the lighthouse there was little room for movement, but John was unwilling to return to one of the lower rooms. He could have retraced his steps to the very bottom of the old building. It would be easier to find the walkie-talkie set now that he had a small torch, but he guessed his brother and the girls would be asleep. There was little to be gained from disturbing them. He was safe where he was and cut off, too, for the sea would be deep around the rocks and the causeway would be well under water by now.

Strangely enough, he had little desire for sleep. The time seemed to pass slowly so he decided to read while he waited for the dawn. He pulled the little Gospel of St. John from his pocket and opened it. He laughed to himself, wondering what his brother would say if he knew what he was doing. But Janet would be pleased. Perhaps she had been praying for him, too.

He had thought little about God since the days when he had attended Sunday school and won several prizes. But as he read afresh the story of how much God loved the world that He sent the Lord Jesus to die on the cross to save us from our sins and that He raised Him from the dead, he remembered words he had heard from his teacher which he thought he had forgotten. There was no doubt of his sin. He admitted that, and he began to feel rather uncomfortable as

F

several incidents came to mind. God had to send His Son to die for sin. It took all the pleasure out of doing wrong, he thought.

Casually, he flicked over the pages, shining his torch so that he could read easily. It all seemed rather strange and the language was old-fashioned, but somehow he couldn't put the book down. There was a lot in it about light and darkness and he remembered what Janet had said about the Bible being so up-to-date. Here he was, sitting in a lighthouse in the dark. In chapter eight he read something which aroused his interest so much that he read it over and over again.

'Then spake Jesus again unto them, saying, I am the light of the world: he that followeth me shall not walk in darkness, but shall have the light of life.'

He switched off his torch. It had become a feeble glow. The Bible talked about a light which wouldn't go out. The light of life!

John shifted his position and decided to go down after all. Somehow, he wasn't afraid of the dark any more. He wanted to shut himself in, away from the lightening sky and the first signs that the darkness of the night would soon disappear. He wanted to pray! As Janet did.

He slid through the hatch and lowered himself into the machinery room and then down into the store-room. Finding the coils of rope, he sat down in the darkness, to talk to the One he couldn't see but who could see him, even in the darkness.

'I've been walking in darkness, Lord Jesus,' John said quietly. 'I've lied, I've cheated, I've stolen, I've laughed at those who follow You, I've wasted my time in wrong things. But You died for sinners. You died for me.'

He paused.

'You know all about my sin,' he continued. 'Please forgive me. I want to leave my sinful ways. I want to follow You from now on. I want to walk in the light which won't go out. Help me, please.'

He listened, hoping his unseen Friend would answer him. But he heard no voice. He sat there for a few more minutes. Why hadn't his new Friend spoken to him? A little disappointed but, at the same time, strangely happy, he went back to the top of the lighthouse.

The pale light of early dawn streaked the sky to the east and, as time went by, John watched the area of light broaden. Soon, the sea reflected the soft yellow glow. A flock of birds, looking tiny in the emptiness of the sky, winged its way towards the mainland. The darkness was retreating!

John felt completely at peace. He hadn't heard a voice but he didn't doubt that his own had been heard or that God had forgiven him. Besides, he reasoned, God had spoken to him through the Bible, and now He was speaking to him through the dawning of a new day, for, as John sat there watching the sky, it reminded him that the darkness of his own life must give way to the light. He hoped God would speak to him often, in different ways. The coming of the dawn was slow. The darkness seemed reluctant to disappear.

When it was quite light and the sea looked like liquid gold beneath him, he went down to recover the walkie-talkie set. He found it under the first tarpaulin he disturbed. Quickly, he raised the aerial and tried to make contact with the cottage. There was no reply.

He looked at his watch. It was just after five o'clock! Of course, they were still asleep!

He pushed the door in vain. There was no means of opening it from the inside, except with a key. He listened for the sound of the sea, but he heard nothing. The quietness was complete. Only the fiercest tempest would be heard inside such a solid structure. The men who had built it so long ago knew their job well.

The lighthouse was still in semi-darkness, especially around the base of the walls where the light from the tiny window slits couldn't penetrate. Only the centre of the floor was undimmed. John's eager eyes quickly discovered a steel trap-door. He tried to lift it, but it was difficult to obtain a good grip with his fingers. In any case, the flap would have been too heavy for him to hold.

'This is where they put the stuff, for sure,' he said aloud. 'I'd love to see what is underneath!'

He glanced around at the tarpaulins which were placed around the walls. Obviously they had covered the whole floor, but the stranger had been so confident nobody would get into the lighthouse that he hadn't bothered to conceal the trap-door.

John smiled to himself. The man might not be a smuggler at all. But in his heart he knew that the strange visitor was up to no good. He had come in the night, because his deeds were evil.

He decided to retreat to his lofty perch by the lantern. After all, it was early enough for the man to return, and if John were caught now it would be disastrous. So, tidying the heavy tarpaulins as best he could, he mounted the stairs.

He looked through the window slits on the way up.

One faced out to sea and the other faced towards Shell Island. But the best view was at the top, and when he gained his vantage point he had a quick look around him. The sea was empty, like the sky, and the island seemed to be asleep.

After another two hours John's set crackled. Immediately, he flicked the switch. Peter was awake at last!

'Are you all right, John?' he asked. 'We've been terribly worried about you!'

John laughed.

'Yes, I'm fine!' he replied, 'though a little hungry. I've been trying to contact you for hours.'

'I've only just woken up,' Peter apologised. 'Just a moment, John. I must tell the girls.'

Peter heaved a great sigh of relief which John heard clearly over the air. Then he yelled at the top of his voice and John put the set at arm's length and turned the volume down.

'It's John! It's John!'

The girls came tumbling into the room in their dressing-gowns.

'Is he all right?' they asked together.

Peter laughed. He felt so relieved.

'Go ahead and ask him,' he said, handing the set to Janet.

Janet spoke into the set and turned up the volume so that they could all hear what John had to tell them.

'Why didn't you contact us last night?' she scolded mildly.

John apologised.

'I had to move very quickly because I thought the man would catch me if I didn't find a place to hide,' he said. 'I couldn't find the spiral staircase first of all, so I hid the set under some tarpaulins so that I could have both hands free. I had just climbed a few stairs when the man returned. Fortunately he didn't hear me. He locked the door and went away. But I couldn't find the set in the dark.'

'Have you tried to get out?' Janet asked.

'Yes. But it's no good. I can't open the door without a key.'

'You must be very hungry by now,' Janet said. 'Can we bring some food along?'

'Rather! As soon as you can, please. There is a room above the stairs which has been used as a store. There are plenty of ropes and I can easily lower one down to you through the little window. Have you a basket? I'll appreciate as much as you can spare.'

'We shall send you the biggest breakfast you have ever had,' Janet said. 'Ann and I will go down to the kitchen now to prepare it, while you tell Peter the rest of the news.'

'Thanks. But just a minute, Janet. I have something special to tell you.'

Janet turned the volume down.

'Go on, tell me,' she whispered.

'I've become a Christian!' John said. 'I know I have! God has forgiven all my sins!'

Janet was over-joyed. At that moment John seemed especially close to her.

'It is what I have prayed for,' she said. 'God is very good, isn't He?'

She gave the set back to Peter.

'What is above the storeroom?' Peter asked when the girls had left the room. 'Look here, John. You really must find a way to get me inside. I'm simply dying to have a look!'

John laughed.

'It's great fun now,' he said, 'but it was a bit lonely during the night. And I am not really looking forward to another night here. I hope Mr. Mortimer comes back soon, although I don't mind the darkness now.'

Peter sighed. 'Unless we can get you out it looks like another lonely night for you, except that we can keep in contact now.'

'So long as the batteries last,' John warned. 'Anyway, I was going to tell you, above the storeroom is a smaller room with all the machinery for working the light. It's fascinating, really. It looks so well maintained, I'm sure the light would work if only I knew what to do! Then above this little room is a ladder leading up to the light itself. There is a marvellous view from here. This morning the rising sun coloured the water yellow and the waves look like little, tiny ripples of gold. I can see the cottage, too, though it is partly screened by trees.'

'Are you up the top now?' Peter asked.

'Yes.'

'Hold on a minute. I'll pop into the other bedroom and wave my handkerchief.'

Peter opened the window of the girls' room and waved. Quite distinctly, he saw his brother, a small figure, peering out from his lofty perch like a bird in a cage.

Peter went back to the set.

'I can see you very clearly,' he said.

'And I can see you. I can see everything from up here, so if our visitor returns I shall be able to tell you.'

John paused for a while.

'I can smell the breakfast cooking,' Peter said, not meaning to tease his brother. 'We'll soon get it up to you. Make sure you have the rope ready.'

'Excellent! I don't think I have ever been so hungry as I am this morning. I'll switch off now. See if the girls have any spare batteries, will you, Peter? They are as important as the food, don't you think?'

Peter agreed.

'We shall be out to you in half an hour or so,' he promised. 'I think there are some spare batteries somewhere. Goodbye for now.'

Peter closed the set and went downstairs. Janet and Ann were putting their breakfasts out on the table. Janet was singing to herself and Peter thought she looked especially happy.

'What did he find in the lighthouse? Gold?' Ann asked.

Peter put his hand to his mouth.

'Do you know? I forgot to ask him!' he said. 'But he says he is quite comfortable. Above the big store-room there is a smaller room which contains the mechanism for working the light. He is right at the top where the lantern is. I waved to him just now.'

'You wait until Uncle comes!' Janet said. 'Won't we have a lot to tell him? And I am sure John would have mentioned it if he had found anything special.'

'I don't think he is looking forward to spending another night on his own, though,' Peter said, thoughtfully. 'Surely there is some way of getting inside.'

Ann shook her head.

'I very much doubt it,' she said. 'These old light-houses were built to keep everything out. I don't think we shall be able to get in.'

While they were preparing John's breakfast they received another message from the lighthouse. John had spotted a small boat heading for the island.

'I don't think they have seen me,' he assured Peter. 'I have come down from the top. I saw them through the window.'

'Good. I'll keep an eye on them and let you know whether they are friends or foes.'

But they turned out to be friends. Two fishermen from the harbour on their way to examine the lobster-pots out to sea had spared the time to make sure that the islanders were in good health and not in need of anything.

Peter hailed them from the jetty.

'Everything is fine,' he lied. 'Any news of Mr. Mortimer?'

'Not yet. Do you want anything today?'

'No, thank you. We have everything we need at the moment.'

Peter hoped they wouldn't call again at a more inconvenient time. If they saw anything suspicious around the foot of the lighthouse they might return and spoil the islanders' chances of solving the mystery.

But the islanders were left to themselves all day. It was quite easy for John to haul up the cardboard carton full of food. The narrow window halfway up the old lighthouse opened stiffly, after he had struggled with it for a few minutes. He threaded the rope through, until it reached the rocks below.

'Be careful how you pull it up,' Ann warned. 'I think you will find all you need inside.'

Gradually, John drew the rope up and then realised, long before the box had reached his level, that the carton would not go through the seven inch wide slit which served as the window.

'I'll tie the rope to the stair rail,' he called to his friends below. 'Then I'll take the things out, one by one.'

It was a slow business, but after a quarter of an hour he had transferred all his supplies, including a note from Janet, from the box to the staircase and up to his observation post on the top of the lighthouse.

'We'll leave you to it, then,' Peter called up. 'Have a good meal. We shall be back presently.'

John waved cheerily.

'Thanks,' he said. 'And don't worry about me. I shall be all right in here.'

They waved back and John's head disappeared inside.

John read Janet's brief letter as he ate his breakfast. Janet had quoted some Scripture. He read it over and over again.

'God is light, and in him is no darkness at all. If we walk in the light, as he is in the light, we have fellowship one with another, and the blood of Jesus Christ his Son cleanseth us from all sin.'

The truth of Scipture brought a warm glow to his heart.

Underneath, she had written a thought of her own.

'You can be God's lighthouse, pointing the way to safety and happiness in Jesus.'

He smiled. Janet had a wonderful way of saying things. God's lighthouse! He liked that! He couldn't walk in the darkness of sin again.

Peter carried the empty carton back to the cottage. Looking back, they saw John at the top of the building steadily munching his breakfast.

Ann looked sad.

'Poor old John,' she said. 'He's a prisoner on our own little island.'

'We are all prisoners, really, I suppose,' Peter replied. 'Prisoners of the sea, until your uncle comes. We can't leave the island unguarded.'

'Oh, I hope he comes today,' Janet said. 'I shall be so glad to see him!'

'And when he comes we shall tell him everything,' Ann said firmly. 'This affair is getting too big for us to handle by ourselves.'

The others agreed. Although they were fond of adventure, it was obvious that the little island had become the centre of a web of mystery. If the visitor returned that night and discovered John, anything could happen.

And this thought kept them subdued all day. While the tide was favourable they spent the time at the foot of the lighthouse, talking to John and sending up all sorts of things he requested. Fortunately, the little cottage seemed to contain everything necessary for an emergency. Soon John was supplied with spare batteries for his walkie-talkie set, a couple of torches, and enough food to keep him in good health for several days. But they couldn't supply what he needed most. He wished they could share the old structure with him. But they couldn't get in.

They tried everything. John came down to the door and tried to budge the lock from the inside while they all pushed from the outside. But the door was built to withstand more than their weight and the two inches of steel which separated them was a barrier which could not be overcome.

'Oh! If only we had a key!' Ann sighed.

In time, of course, they had to leave the causeway. The tide had a timetable to keep. It could not be delayed. It crept along the stonework and cascaded on to the rocks below. Soon the sea was breaking against the lighthouse walls and they understood why it had to be built so solidly.

'The sun has disappeared,' Ann said shivering a little, in spite of the warm air.

'And there will be a heavy sea if this breeze gets any stronger,' Peter observed. 'Just look at the waves!'

They kept in touch with John all day. He hadn't found any loot in the lighthouse, although he had searched it from top to bottom. There was no apparent reason for the mysterious nightly visits. But, tired as he was, John was determined to keep awake so that he could observe all that took place below, if the stranger returned.

CHAPTER 10

The stranger did return! It was one of those warm, wild nights when every leaf on the island rustled in the darkness. A night to make you wonder at the soft noises which seemed to infect the whole island. A night fit for excitement. A night to remember!

John spotted the boat from his lofty perch at about ten o'clock, when it had been dark for nearly an hour. Immediately, he contacted the others in the cottage.

'It's a bigger boat this time,' he said quite calmly. 'I think it is going to tie up at the jetty. What a nerve these people have!'

The others were dressed in their warmest clothes, for each of them thought secretly that the night would be an eventful one. Not one of them had thought of going to bed.

'We'll slip out of the cottage quietly,' Peter told his brother. 'I shall be near the causeway and the girls will be hidden in the bushes. Take great care the men don't see you, John, and don't call me back unless you really have to.'

Janet closed the door quietly. With hearts thumping and a dry feeling in their mouths, they crept out into the shadow of the bushes to await the arrival of their visitors.

The boat was a long, black shape on the dark sea, and, when the moon broke through the scudding clouds for a moment, they caught a glimpse of a man standing in the bows as the sleek vessel nosed its way silently towards the jetty. Only the low hum of the diesel engine betrayed its presence. If they had been in the cottage, they would never have known that their visitors had arrived.

'I wonder who they are,' Janet whispered.

It was hard to tell in the dark.

They watched silently. Peter thought there were at least three men, but it was difficult to be sure because the visitors kept jumping down into the boat from the jetty and then climbing up more slowly with packages in their hands.

'They are unloading something,' Peter whispered to the girls who were huddled close beside him. 'I wonder what it is.'

'They seem very efficient, anyway,' Ann said. 'They haven't uttered one word yet, and they know exactly what to do.'

'Are we quite safe here?' Janet asked, a little nervously. 'They won't discover us, will they?'

'Not if we keep still.'

Peter's voice reassured her and Janet took comfort.

'I wish poor old John wasn't in the lighthouse, though,' she murmured.

Another gap in the clouds allowed the moon to shine through and they had a clearer view of the jetty. There was a fair sized pile of packages heaped on the jetty and, by the way the men were working, it was clear that the packages were quite heavy.

'Gold?' whispered Ann.

Peter shook his head.

'I doubt it,' he said. 'Why bring it here?'

Janet was just about to express an opinion when they heard a low murmur of voices, and then one of the men walked towards them.

Janet's fingernails dug deep into Peter's arm and in other circumstances he would have cried out. But it was essential that they kept their presence a secret. The man hadn't seen them, however. He walked along the beach in front of them, taking his time, as if he were used to an evening stroll before going to bed. But he was making for the lighthouse.

Peter bit his lip.

'I'll warn John,' he whispered. 'He may not have noticed.'

Quickly and silently, he extended the aerial while the girls kept an eye on the other men on the jetty. A cigarette glowed in the darkness. The men were resting after their strenuous labours.

'Are you there, John?'

Peter held the set right against his mouth and hoped his brother would hear him.

'Yes.'

John's voice sounded high-pitched and excited.

'One of the men is coming your way,' Peter warned. 'Keep well out of sight and don't do anything rash.'

There was a slight pause.

'All right,' John replied. 'Look after yourselves, too. And don't worry about me. Remember Mr. Mortimer may be here tomorrow.'

Tomorrow! Peter wished it were tomorrow, today!

'Can you hear anything yet?' he asked. 'All is quiet this end. The men are resting after unloading the boat.'

'No sound yet.'

There was another pause. Peter imagined his brother straining his ears for the sound which would tell him the lighthouse was about to be entered.

'Now! Yes! I can hear somebody at the door! Goodbye, Peter. I'm closing down.'

There was silence.

Reluctantly, Peter switched off his set and turned his attention to the men on the jetty. But the moon had retreated behind the clouds and it was difficult to see clearly again.

'Is John all right?' Janet asked quietly. 'I mean, is there anything we can do to help?'

'It does seem rather pointless just sitting here,' Ann whispered.

Peter smiled, in spite of their difficult position. The girls had recovered from the first shock of seeing the men on the island, and their courage had returned.

'I hope the other man will leave the lighthouse door open when he returns to the boat. It would be easy for John to slip out and rejoin us. The darkness is almost complete,' he replied.

'Then go along and see what you can do,' Janet pleaded. 'We shall be quite safe here and you will know where to find us when you return.'

Peter looked doubtful. True, they were safe all the while they kept quite still, but would they be able to stay for very long in their cramped position?

Ann nudged him.

'Go on, then,' she said quite calmly. 'We shall be all right. And you will be able to tell John when the coast is clear.'

Peter gripped their hands.

'You are a brave pair,' he said. 'I won't be long.'

Carefully, he crept out of their hiding place. His plimsolled feet trod the sloping ground silently and he was able to curl up his toes inside whenever he was in danger of slipping. He decided not to risk walking along the beach, certainly the easier way to the causeway. But the clouds were treacherous and the moon fickle. He dare not risk discovery when the moon decided to peep down. He shuddered at the thought. He wasn't worried for his own safety, but what would the girls do if both he and John were held prisoner? He took extra care where he put his feet.

At last he reached a spot about ten feet above the level of the beach by the causeway. The lighthouse was nearly invisible in the darkness, except where the soft pink glow shone through the lower window. The man was still inside and the door was shut. Peter tried to make up his mind whether to creep along the causeway and hide at the foot of the lighthouse or to stay secure in his hiding place.

Wisely, he decided to stay put, and, after making that decision, he knew he had done the right thing. He calculated that it would have taken a minute to reach the lighthouse. In less than that time, quite suddenly the door opened and the man came out. If Peter had decided on the first course of action he would have been caught on the doorstep!

Thankfulness quickly turned to disappointment, though, as the stranger locked the door behind him, before tramping down the causeway in his rubber boots. Peter could have jumped down on to his shoulders as he passed along the beach directly beneath him. Once the man stumbled and cursed quietly. Then Peter knew he wasn't a local fisherman. He was a foreigner!

He waited until the man was halfway along the beach before calling John on the set.

John was pleased to hear his brother's voice.

G

'I wish you were here, Peter,' he said.

His voice betrayed his great excitement.

'Can you see anything now?'

'Yes! The man left the hurricane-lamp alight and I crept halfway down the stairs for a close look. There is a large tank beneath the floor! It looks like a fresh water tank from here. The man opened it up and I could hear him panting with the effort of moving the hinged trap-doors. There isn't anything inside—at least, I can't see anything from here—but it is a perfect hiding place.'

'How big is it, then?'

'Oh, I should say about five feet square. I don't know how deep it is because the inside is in the shadows.'

'They will be coming back soon,' Peter said. 'Look, John, if the coast is clear and they leave the door open when they go backwards and forwards along the beach, I'll tell you when to creep out along the causeway. If you bend almost double, there is a good chance you won't be discovered. I shall be much happier if you are outside the lighthouse.'

'All right. We have only to remain undetected and perhaps the men will go away again. The stuff will be safe and we can tell the police or the customs men when Mr. Mortimer comes. Can you see any movement at the other end of the beach, Peter?'

'I can hardly see a thing,' Peter admitted. 'I think we had better lie low now. The men may be coming along the beach, for all I know.'

'Goodbye, then,' John said. 'And don't forget to let me know if I can make a dash for it.'

'I won't forget,' Peter assured him. 'I'm directly above the causeway, about ten feet up, that's all.'

He switched off and listened. The only sound was the regular swish of the waves upon the shore and the gentle rustle of the leaves above him. Although he couldn't see clearly, he was thankful for the darkness. It was his protection. If he stayed where he was he was perfectly secure. He hoped the girls would do the same.

But the girls were getting restless. The man returned from the lighthouse and they watched while he instructed the other men quietly. Then, the men began to pick up the heavy packages and stumble along the jetty. One by one, they passed the girls and disappeared into the darkness.

'It will take them a good ten minutes to carry those to the lighthouse,' Ann whispered. 'Let's have a look at the other packages on the jetty. It is quite safe.'

'Yes! I'm fed up with sitting here doing nothing. We mustn't let the boys have all the fun.'

Janet was ready for an adventure.

'But we must be careful,' Ann warned. 'Peter would be very cross if we were discovered.'

Hand in hand, they crept across the beach. It was only a few yards to the jetty and they trod lightly along to the boat. Bending down, they felt the packages.

'They are all sewn up in canvas,' Ann whispered. 'Whatever can they contain?'

They tried to turn the packages over and, in making the attempt, Janet allowed one of the heaviest containers to drop on Ann's foot.

'Ouch!'

Ann sat down on the jetty and rubbed her toes vigorously.

'Oh, I am sorry!'

Janet was anxious lest the heavy parcel had damaged her sister's toes.

'I shall feel all right in a minute,' Ann assured her. 'Then we must get back in hiding, in case the men return.'

'Ye . . . es.'

Janet felt a sudden tingling of her spine. Although her back was towards the boat, somehow she knew, instinctively, that they were not alone. She wanted to turn around but she was unable to move!

Ann looked up at her, puzzled.

'It's all right, Janet,' she said. 'I'm not that bad. You needn't worry. My foot feels much . . .'

Her voice trailed off into thin air. A man was standing right behind Janet.

'I think you two had better come over to the lighthouse,' the sailor said in broken English. 'You will feel a lot safer there!'

He grabbed Ann's arm and hoisted her to her feet. Then, turning quickly, he faced Janet.

'If you had any thoughts about escaping,' he warned, 'I should forget them.'

Then, seeing the look of alarm on Janet's face, he spoke less harshly.

'You will not come to any harm with me,' he said.

CHAPTER 11

Over at the lighthouse the men were busy. Peter, keeping watch from his observation post, saw every move the men made. They stacked the containers on the causeway at the foot of the lighthouse steps. He noted how carefully they handled them and guessed that the contents were fragile as well as heavy. The lighthouse door was wide open and he could see part of the interior. He wondered if his brother was watching from high up inside the tower. There was no chance of John escaping while the men were active below, for packages were being carried in every half minute or so. The doorway was narrow and, agile as John was, he could not hope to avoid detection.

Peter shifted his position slightly, to a spot where he could raise the aerial without danger of its being trapped in the branches which drooped low over the ground. The moon was still hidden by clouds. He looked at his watch. It was just after eleven.

Suddenly, his attention was attracted by the sound of rubber boots on the causeway again. He withdrew further into the bushes. The leader of the group was outlined in the doorway for a brief moment. They were taking no chances. The lighthouse would not be left unguarded.

Peter was bitterly disappointed. It would have been good to have helped John to escape, not least for the company he would provide. As twins, they were much closer than many brothers and he would have been much happier if John had been with him. He decided to risk calling him on the set. The other men were somewhere along the beach, on their way back to the jetty for another load of packages. The leader was inside the lighthouse, out of sight.

He relaxed a little when he heard his brother's voice again in response to his call.

'I am right at the top now,' John said. 'I don't think there is much chance of making an escape, do you?'

Peter sighed.

'I'm afraid not, John,' he replied. 'The best thing to do is to lie low and make sure you are not discovered. Stay at the top. The men are unlikely to go up there if they don't suspect anything.'

'It will soon be tomorrow,' John said, cheerfully. 'I think you ought to go back to the girls. Tell them I am quite safe.'

Peter grinned.

'All right, John,' he said. 'I'll tell them. We shall keep well out of sight, too. If the men don't suspect anything they will go away before dawn. They dare not leave the boat here after first light, in case they arouse suspicion.'

'Goodbye,' John said.

Peter retracted the aerial and began to move stealthily through the bushes, like a cat. He wished he had a cat's eyesight. The night was as black as tar.

Although their time on the island had been short, Peter felt he knew every inch of it. They had scrambled into every nook and cranny. Peter knew when he would pass the cottage, but if he hadn't been aware of its situation he could easily have missed it. The house was in darkness, of course.

He approached the jetty area with extreme caution. He didn't want to frighten the girls by suddenly appearing out of the blackness. He decided to risk whispering a recognition signal to them when he was a few yards away. He hoped they wouldn't jump out of their skins and give away their position to the men on the beach.

But when Peter arrived at the spot there was no sign of Janet and Ann. Deeply puzzled, he checked his position by comparing the angle of the jetty with the boat, which he could just see against the lighter background of the water. This was the spot, all right. But all was deathly quiet. The men must have gone off with another load. There was no sign of anybody.

Peter hoped the girls had merely withdrawn further up the hillside. He decided to try to find them. Carefully, he climbed the hill, calling softly. Soon, he was right up on the ridge. A light beckoned across the water from the mainland. The rest of the world seemed to be in complete darkness. He began to retrace his steps down the hill towards the beach. Suddenly, he heard a crackle from his set. John was on the air.

'Can you hear me, Peter?'

Peter flicked the switch over and replied.

'Yes.'

'Listen carefully. I'm right at the top of the lighthouse on my own. The girls are in the service room just below me.'

'The girls!'

Peter's voice betrayed his alarm.

'I'm sorry, Peter. I thought you knew. They were captured by the jetty and brought in here. Fortunately, I was hidden behind some machinery so the men didn't see me. They have no idea that I am here or that there are any others on the island. The girls didn't give the game away.'

Suddenly, John went off the air.

'Oh dear! What a spot we are in now!'

Peter spoke aloud. He felt so worried. If only the girls had heeded his warning and stayed in the shelter of the undergrowth, they would not have been in this dangerous situation. Peter thought hard. Was there anything he could do?

He retraced his steps to the ridge and looked across the water to the mainland. The light had gone out. To see that again would have been a comfort. He felt right at the end of his tether. The struggle seemed so unequal. He began to wish that he had been captured, too. He longed for friendly company for, out here, he was alone. He didn't know the Friend John knew, the One who would have helped him most of all.

He stood on the ridge, bracing himself against the wind which whistled through his hair and made the trees dance in the darkness. At that moment his set buzzed. Greatly encouraged, he switched on.

'Sorry about the long interval,' John apologised. 'The men came up to see what the girls were doing. They seem to be treating them quite well. One of the men gave them a bar of chocolate. Janet passed half of it up to me.'

'Stop making me feel hungry,' Peter said.

'Anyway,' John continued, 'the men haven't realised that Janet and Ann speak perfect French. They listened while the leader discussed the situation with the others. He plans to leave the island before first light and he means to take the girls with him,

possibly back to France! He doesn't want them on
the island when the local contacts call for the stuff. I
suppose he thinks they might recognise some of the
gang.'

'What do you suggest?' Peter asked.

'You must immobilise their boat,' John replied.
'That is the only way to stop them. Then we are all
prisoners on the island and we shall be on level terms,
until Mr. Mortimer comes.'

'That might be today!' Peter said, looking at his
watch which glowed in the darkness. 'It is already
after midnight. Besides, one of the fishermen might
call. If he does, I'll swim out to him. We can bring
the police.'

'Good! Now, please be very careful. And contact
me as soon as you have dealt with the boat. No! Don't
do that. They may have found me by then.'

'All right. If you don't contact me at two o'clock, I
shall know you have been caught. Keep the girls'
spirits high.'

'I shall,' John promised. 'God is with us!'

Peter looked thoughtful. John had never said anything like that before. Strangely encouraged, he began to walk down the hill.

Peter had no idea how he was going to render the
boat useless. The little he knew about boats had been
learned on this holiday when he had been aboard
Mariner. Mr. Mortimer had explained to him, in
simple terms, how the engine worked. But *Mariner*
wasn't a diesel powered vessel. He wondered if there
would be a plug in the bottom of the boat which he
could unscrew, allowing the craft to fill with water
slowly, while he jumped to safety. He felt it would be
wrong to do any permanent damage to the boat, but

it would be quite a different matter to sink it in the six feet of water which slapped the jetty at low tide. A small crane could lift the vessel out of the water, undamaged.

These were his thoughts as he reached the beach and paused awhile in the darkness to listen for any unfamiliar sounds. All he heard was the sea and the wind in the trees. The tide was coming in again. Suddenly, he realised that the men would have to bring the girls back to the jetty within the hour, otherwise the causeway would be covered by the sea. Gritting his teeth, he bent low and raced across the beach.

Peter stepped on to the long, sleek craft warily, ready to turn tail and flee back along the jetty to the safety of the trees. A light was burning in the galley. He opened the door a couple of inches and peeped through. As far as he could tell, the vessel was unoccupied. Becoming bolder, he crept through the boat from bow to stern. The crew were all in the lighthouse!

For a moment he thought of starting the engine and sailing away to the harbour for help. If it had been *Mariner* he might have been successful, although he doubted whether he could find the harbour entrance in the darkness. He reckoned he could handle a small cruiser, but this was a different matter. The engine was much more powerful, of greater range, and he had no idea how to make it useless. Frustrated, he sat on a locker to think. How could he prevent the men taking the girls away?

He wandered aft. He discovered a small toilet and, behind this, a large steel tank surrounded by a heap of cotton waste. The tank reeked of oil. Of course, this was the answer! He wouldn't have to damage the boat at all. The vessel wouldn't function without any fuel!

With some difficulty, he disconnected a pipe which ran from the tank to the engine. The thick black liquid poured all over his plimsolls and he slid around trying to find a bucket to collect the precious fuel in. An empty oil drum stood by the engine and he slithered back with that and placed it under the glistening, smelly river. The oil splashed into the empty drum and he knew that anybody within half a mile could not fail to hear. He lifted the drum to the level of the stern and poured the oil on to the sea. He repeated the process seven times before he heard shouts along the beach and he reckoned it was time to leave. In any case, the job was done, for just as he looked around for a way of escape, the last of the oil gurgled out of the drum on to the floor. Without a moment's hesitation, Peter stood on the stern and dived straight through the ugly black patch which was spreading over a wide area. Holding his breath, he swam away beneath the surface.

The water was cool and pleasant. Peter felt so happy that if he had not been afraid of betraying his position he would have sung out loud. The oil smelt terrible, and he swam quickly into clearer water and floated on his back. He listened with amusement to the consternation he had caused. He could hear the men slipping and sliding all over the vessel, getting more angry with each other every minute. Chuckling to himself, he swam quietly away.

He had left his walkie-talkie set by the spring so he had no difficulty in recovering it. Trembling with excitement, he called his brother, not bothering to wait for John to contact him. Quite rightly, he reckoned that, in the general pandemonium, nobody would bother about the prisoners, particularly the one they hadn't discovered!

'I've done it!' he said.

John laughed.

'I should think you have! You've caused more confusion in the last few minutes than most people cause all their lives!'

'I ditched all their fuel,' Peter explained. 'They won't be able to sail now.'

'Well done!'

John's voice came loud and clear over the air. And then, to Peter's dismay, his brother's voice trailed off.

'I've been seen, Peter! It's up to you now!'

Peter listened but no other sound came. He hoped John would have kept his set switched on so that he would have some clue as to what had happened. But there was no contact. Perhaps his brother had hidden the set under some equipment before it was discovered.

Peter decided to be extra careful. The men would be more than annoyed, and the leader, who would be furious at the way he had been tricked, was bound to order a search of the whole island, if only for the satisfaction of bringing the culprit into the lighthouse.

But time was on Peter's side. As the men tramped wearily along the beach back to the safety of the old building, Peter, who had moved swiftly over to the causeway, counted them as they waded through the water and climbed the steps to the door. One. Two. Three. And one inside, of course. Everybody was in the lighthouse, and the tide was already cascading off the walls of the causeway very near the shore.

It was at this point that Peter realised he was very tired—and hungry. He decided to go back to the cottage to cook himself a meal. He would keep an eye open in case any of the men had the idea of venturing forth from their citadel, but he guessed that, dispirited as they must be, they would prefer to remain dry and warm until the tide allowed them to come out at about seven o'clock in the morning. For a few hours, at least, he was perfectly safe.

CHAPTER 12

The first thing Peter did when he reached the cottage was to wriggle out of his wet clothes and have a wash. There wasn't a bathroom in the little house but the kitchen window faced away from the lighthouse and Peter thought it quite safe to switch on a powerful torch. Looking in the mirror, he realised what a mess he was in. Traces of oil clung to his hair and circled his face. It was with some difficulty that he made himself look presentable again. His eyes looked red and tired, but he knew he dare not go to bed in case he did not awake early in the morning. So he ate instead.

He fumbled in the darkness for the little store of tinned food they kept outside under a tarpaulin. He grunted his satisfaction when he discovered that the first tin he pulled out was chicken in gravy. He wondered whether he ought to open it. After all, this was their prize tin and it was a pity not to share it. But hunger got the better of him, and, knowing his friends would not disapprove, he emptied the contents of the can into a saucepan and put it on the cooker. He stirred the mixture with a wooden spoon, leaning low over the saucepan to catch the delicious aroma.

Peter decided to eat in the kitchen, too. It was better than sitting in the darkness in the other room. He heard the wind outside and pictured the sea around the lighthouse. He felt warm and secure. The men would surely search for him in the morning. But it was only two o'clock and he had several hours of freedom.

In spite of his efforts to keep awake, sleep overcame him. He awoke with a start and realised that the darkness had gone. He wondered what had woken him and he listened carefully for any suspicious noise. All he heard was the twittering of the birds and, because the window was open, the sound of the sea, a far away gentle sound which soothed him. He loved to listen to the sea. He glanced at his watch; it was half past six. Time to leave the cottage. Time to hide up the hill.

He packed a small haversack of food and took one of the smaller water containers. First he would call at the spring and afterwards find an observation point where he could see most of the island yet remain hidden himself.

The water from the spring was clear and cool. It sparkled in the early morning sunshine as it bubbled from the deep parts of the earth. Peter was grateful for the spring. He wondered how many sailors, shipwrecked perhaps, in years gone by, had drunk the icy waters and been refreshed by them. He splashed the water over his face and dried himself on his handkerchief. He felt better equipped now for what might lay before him. He knew that the day would be demanding and, if he were to outwit the searchers, he would need to keep a cool head.

He lay down just beyond the skyline and looked across the water to *Sea Breezes*. It looked so near, near enough to swim. But Peter knew how strong the current was between the island and the mainland. Besides, he doubted whether he could swim three miles.

The cliff sloped down quite steeply to the rocks below. He wondered whether he dare scramble down if he were hard pressed and doubted if he could climb up again. His purpose wasn't just to avoid capture but to summon help. He was thinking how he might do this when his set crackled and he flicked the switch. It was John.

'Are you all right?' Peter asked.

'Fine!'

John sounded cheerful and confident.

'Where are you now?'

'We are all in the service room below the lantern. The girls are here and they want to have a word with you, too.'

'Hello, Peter.'

It was good to hear her voice again.

'Hello, Ann. Your uncle might come back today.'

'Yes. And if he does you must warn him not to land on the island.'

Peter grinned.

'Easier said than done,' he observed. 'What do you suggest?'

'I mustn't speak too loudly and if I switch off suddenly you will know that the seaman who slept in this room has woken at last. They captured John, but he managed to hide the set and they don't know we have it. We haven't been badly treated but I think they are very angry about your exploits. Please be careful, Peter. If they catch you they might do anything.'

'I'll be careful,' Peter promised.

'Janet wants to speak to you now.'

'Hello, Peter.'

'Hello.'

'I have a strong feeling Uncle will come today and

we might be able to help you warn him before he arrives. Will you contact us on the set when he rounds the headland? I believe we have found out how to work the foghorn in here. If we can keep the guard busy for half a minute we may be able to do it.'

'Great! But will your uncle realise something is up?'

Janet laughed.

'He could hardly fail to,' she said. 'The beach is strewn with oil and a strange ship is tied up at the jetty, unable to sail.'

Peter felt good.

'I'm sorry about the beach,' he apologised. 'But I didn't want them to take you back to France. It's a long trip and I know what rotten sailors you are!'

'You just wait!'

Then, suddenly, the set went lifeless and Peter guessed that the guard was stirring into life.

They didn't come for him until nine o'clock. Peter had begun to think that they were resigned to being arrested and they would leave him alone, but his thoughts in that direction were quickly dispelled when he saw three burly men climbing the hill towards him.

Peter lay quite still, watching them for over an hour searching fruitlessly for their prey. Then the leading man approached the ridge about fifty yards to the east of Peter. He was thick set and in his hand he carried a stick with which he beat the undergrowth as he walked. The others were younger and not so purposeful. In fact, the last of the trio looked decidedly fed up! Then, quite suddenly, they turned westwards to walk along the ridge. Peter knew they would discover him if he remained where he was.

H

Now was the time to move!

He left his haversack in the bushes and, clutching the set tightly, he moved, crablike, down the hill towards the beach, at an angle away from the men. He hoped they wouldn't see him. For a moment he remained undetected but a sudden shout told him he had been discovered. The chase was on!

They chased him all over the island. They tried to force him into a position where their superior numbers would make it impossible for him to escape. But Peter was as agile as a cat, and lightly clad. On more than one occasion they nearly captured him. Indeed, twice his pursuers caught hold of his sleeve, but a quick twist of the arm enabled Peter to wriggle free. At midday the men decided to call off the chase for a while.

Peter sat down just below the ridge and watched them, warily. They sat under the trees arguing among themselves. Peter noticed they had eased their hot feet from their rubber boots. For a moment he considered whether he could dart in and snatch their boots away from them, but he decided against this. He had a drink at the spring and splashed the cool water over his face. This refreshed him again. He had held the walkie-talkie set tightly all through the chase and he decided to call up John to assure them he was all right, but he couldn't obtain any reply. He hoped the others were not worrying too much about him. Then he hid the set, for he didn't want it to be damaged. After all, Mr. Mortimer had entrusted it to their care. He reckoned the men would try to drive him into the sea when they resumed the chase. He found an ideal spot and secretly marked the place. When he looked across at the men again, they were just beginning to walk towards him.

The sun blazed down upon the little island. The trees were still. The sea, a smooth mass of deep blue, looked invitingly cool. Peter decided to allow the men to chase him into the sea, for he knew they must capture him eventually, unless he took to the water. His mind made up, he scrambled down the hill.

He plunged off the jetty just as they stumbled across the beach. Peter trod water a little way off and then swam around the headland. Not one of the men thought of following him. Clearly, he was quite safe in the sea. But he couldn't see what was happening. So he pulled himself out of the water on the western side of the island and climbed up to the knife edge ridge where he could observe everything.

Peter looked for the men but he couldn't see them at first. Then he spotted them behind the jetty half hidden from the bay. They seemed to be peering intently over the concrete. When Peter followed the direction with his own eyes, he realised what they were looking at. *Mariner* was passing the lighthouse and was heading for the jetty! Mr. Mortimer had come the other way!

Desperately, Peter ran to the spot where he had hidden the set. With trembling hands he extended the aerial. He screamed into it.

'John! The foghorn!'

But it wasn't John who replied. Instead, another voice came over the air.

'Don't worry, my friend,' it said, in broken English. 'The foghorn will not sound today.'

Peter felt like bursting into tears. It seemed that all his valiant efforts had been of little use. He had delayed the time of departure of the smugglers, but he had failed in his main purpose of warning Mr. Mortimer. He watched, helplessly, as the men boarded *Mariner* and brought the architect out. Two of them led him along the beach to the lighthouse while the third stood guard over the little red cruiser. They were not taking any more chances!

Peter wrung his hands in despair.

'Why didn't you see the oil?' he called out.

But they were too far along the beach to hear him. Peter sunk to the ground, utterly dejected. Suddenly he felt very tired.

He guessed Mr. Mortimer would be locked in the lighthouse while two of the men took *Mariner* to a point along the coast where the vessel wasn't well known. They must have their contacts on the mainland who would supply them with enough diesel fuel for the return trip to France. He expected they would take their captives with them. He doubted whether they would come to any harm but, if the loot was valuable, the smugglers could not risk any further upset before the local men came to take it away. Wearily, he picked up the set and moved down the hill nearer the beach.

He didn't have to wait long. Two men came out of the lighthouse and strode across the sands. Peter bit his lip as they boarded *Mariner* and the other man who had been on guard started back to the lighthouse. He watched the craft glide out from the jetty and disappear around the headland. On a sudden impulse, he scrambled up the hill again to see which way they would go. To his surprise he saw that they were heading straight for the harbour. Then they changed course, westwards.

Peter stood up and shook his fist angrily at the men.

It was a hopeless gesture. Even if they could see him they would only laugh at him. All his defiance and determination would not prevent them from sailing away, leaving him alone, a prisoner of the sea. Only a miracle could prevent that from happening. And Peter didn't believe in miracles. He had done his best and it hadn't been good enough. When, after some while, he saw *Mariner* sailing in, his dejection was complete.

But over at the lighthouse they were in good heart. John and Janet had spent hours discussing John's new-found faith and encouraging one another from the Gospel they read. Even Ann listened with some interest although, secretly she planned to resist any attempt to influence her. She wanted to run her own life as she pleased. However, she had to admit that she had never seen John so happy, not even when he had seen the island for the very first time.

The arrival of Mr. Mortimer had been a further encouragement.

'They won't get away with this,' he told the young people. 'I think they are more nervous than ourselves!'

And so it seemed. The men were definitely on edge. They argued among themselves and strode up and down, waiting for their oil supply from the mainland. Two of the men were in favour of staying on the island to see the loot safely away. John wondered why they did not keep in different pairs. It would certainly save a lot of harsh words. But perhaps the leader didn't trust the others. The other two wanted to sail with their captives as quickly as possible. It would be easy to cruise for a few hours and to bring the prisoners back after dark.

'Perhaps the leader is wise to keep the like-minded ones apart,' John said. 'They might have sailed away without coming back for their so-called friends!'

'They don't mean to harm us, anyway,' Janet said.

John grinned.

'I think they have taken on more than they can manage,' he whispered. 'God is with us!'

'So we shall win!' Janet exclaimed. 'Oh, I'm so happy you have become a Christian, too!'

Mariner was not left unguarded. One man stayed behind while his companion hurried along the beach to tell the others the vessel was ready for the voyage. The tide had begun to slop over the causeway already. Their journey would begin with wet feet!

It seemed ages before they emerged from the light-house. Peter imagined all sorts of horrible things. Perhaps there was a struggle because the captives had refused to co-operate with the seamen. Perhaps John had barricaded himself in at the top and was refusing to move, But, looking across the bay to the lantern, Peter could see right through the glass.

At the jetty the man guarding *Mariner* was becoming impatient, too. Peter watched him puffing nervously at a cigarette. He saw him throw the stub into the sea and light another.

Then, suddenly, Peter noticed another vessel. It was a big and black. He didn't have to be an expert to recognise the business-like lines of the revenue cutter, even though it was at least three miles away. Quickly, he extended his aerial to its maximum height and spoke into the set.

'Emergency on Shell Island! Islanders being held prisoner by smugglers! Please help! At once!'

He repeated the message over and over again, hoping the island would be marked on the captain's chart. Hoping he was in range of the delicate instruments. Hoping.

Conditions were perfect for transmitting and receiving. The sea was calm. There were no obstructions. On board, the radio operator was slowly twisting the controls of his powerful receiver. He was on listening watch. Suddenly, he adjusted his headphones and listened more intently. Then, without looking up, he called his officer. In a moment the captain was scanning Shell Island through powerful binoculars. It was easy to pinpoint the vessels at the old jetty. And the oil still lay in patches on the surface of the sea. He altered course immediately.

Peter knew nothing of what was happening aboard the cutter. The vessel appeared to be proceeding as before. The bow wave looked small and from such a distance it was impossible to tell if the cutter had altered course. So Peter continued to transmit. Then the party emerged from the lighthouse.

He wondered if there would be a struggle. John was being dragged unwillingly along the causeway and, when they came to the far end, the men nearly threw him down the steps. Mr. Mortimer's hands were tied behind his back and a tight hold was kept on the girls. Clearly, the men were not taking any risks.

Peter was unwilling to see his friends leave the island without a fight. He was very angry and he decided to see what he could do. He ran down the hill on to the beach where the group was making slow progress towards the jetty. He approached them quickly, putting as much ground between them and their goal. If one of the men tried to grab him, the smuggler would have to relax his grip for a moment. And John would be free!

The leader of the gang, realising Peter's plan, shouted a warning. But he was too late. As Peter darted in, the smuggler relaxed his hold and John twisted away to join his brother. Now, quite easily, two of them were free.

With angry scowls and loud curses the men hustled the remainder of their prisoners along the beach. The guard on the jetty ran back to help his leader deal with the architect, who was making things as difficult as possible in spite of his bonds. In all the excitement, none of them noticed that the cutter had moored in the bay and a high speed launch was racing towards them.

They were only aware of the turn of events when a helicopter, summoned by the captain of the cutter, clattered over the hill and dipped down towards them.

Peter and John danced wildly along the beach with delight. The exit door of the machine was open, and, as it hovered low over the jetty, three coastguards slid down a rope with practised skill. At that moment, too, the launch arrived.

The seamen looked sullen and, suddenly, small. The islanders looked very happy. The customs men looked puzzled.

'Would anyone care to explain?' their leader said.

CHAPTER 13

The helicopter had left. The cutter had resumed its voyage down channel towards Plymouth with the smugglers in safe custody aboard. All was quiet on the island again.

'What will happen to them?' Ann asked.

Mr. Mortimer shook his head.

'I don't know for sure,' he replied. 'They may escape with a heavy fine, depending on the value of the loot and whether this is their first offence or not. They may go to prison for a time, but probably not for long.'

'At least they didn't ill-treat us,' Janet said. 'And it was very exciting, wasn't it?'

'You all behaved splendidly,' the architect said. 'And especially you, Peter. We might have been in France now, but for your brave efforts.'

Peter smiled.

'But why didn't you turn back when you saw the oil?' he asked. 'And the other boat was there, too.'

Mr. Mortimer laughed.

'I have been asking that question of myself. I suppose I was inquisitive—and very worried. After all, it is my island and you are my guests. I had to look after you, didn't I?'

They all laughed.

'The revenue men told me they have been trying to catch this gang for several months,' John said. 'They knew they operated somewhere along this coast

but the smugglers were very clever at avoiding capture. They said a larger boat anchors a few miles out
to sea and the smaller vessel ferries the loot to and
fro.'

'Will the customs men keep the loot?' Peter asked.

He was thinking of the watches and cameras and
heavier articles which were safely locked in the lighthouse again.

'And how did the men get a key?' asked John.

'The customs will impound the goods,' the architect replied. 'They will be used as evidence in court
first, of course. The key was made by a craftsman. It
fitted perfectly!'

'What a pity men waste their talents in trying to
obtain more money, illegally,' Ann remarked.

'And the local men?' Janet enquired.

'May never be caught! The gang are unlikely to
say who their contacts are. They may even try to run
the gauntlet again, when they are free! Smugglers are
persistent people, you know.'

'Do you think there is any chance of catching the
others? Will they come to collect the stuff?'

Peter was looking for more adventure already.

'Not a chance!' Mr. Mortimer replied. 'News
travels fast, even in these sleepy parts. The townsfolk
will have noticed the helicopter and the cutter. No, it
is my opinion that we shall never know who else was
involved with the gang.'

'I am glad our other visitor wasn't mixed up in this
nasty business,' Janet said. 'But he could hardly
blame us for being suspicious first of all.'

'Henry is as honest as you are,' Mr. Mortimer replied. 'He wouldn't have anything to do with smugg-
ling.'

They finished their tea and cleared up for the customs men who were to sleep in the cottage that night. Others were to guard the lighthouse in case the local men arrived, but it was a slender hope.

As they walked down to the jetty where *Mariner* bobbed on the waves, John was at Janet's side. A smile spread over his face as he remembered God's goodness to him and to the others.

'A penny for your thoughts,' laughed Janet.

'They couldn't be valued in money,' John replied slowly, 'for I was thinking how kind it was of God to make sure that we came to no harm. After all, lots could have happened to us.'

'Yes.' Janet looked serious. 'I do thank Him for keeping us all safe and for sending you His light, right up there in that dark old lighthouse.'

'God's word came to me in the darkness, and I know now that my future is in His hands, for I have told Him that I want to follow Him—always.'

Then Peter's voice reached them as he said, 'So it's back to *Sea Breezes*. I thought at one time I should have to stay here for ever. On my own!'

They all laughed. It was good to be together again. Even good to be leaving the island they loved—just for a couple of days.